# MARK MANNOCK

# KILLSONG

*A Nicholas Sharp Thriller (1)*

*First published by Shotfire Books 2020*

*This novel is entirely a work of fiction. The names, characters and incidents portrayed in it are the work of the author's imagination. Any resemblance to actual persons, living or dead, events or localities is entirely coincidental.*

*Mark Mannock asserts the moral right to be identified as the author of this work.*

*First edition*

*ISBN: 978-0-6489036-0-4*

*This book was professionally typeset on Reedsy.
Find out more at reedsy.com*

*For John*

The only thing necessary for the triumph of evil is that good men do nothing...for Nicholas Sharp, doing nothing is not an option.

# Contents

# Chapter 1

The explosive roar shattered the night air. A split second later a blinding white light arced across the sky, turning night into day.

Close your eyes and you heard a hundred jet engines. Open them and you saw twenty-five thousand people in a full-volume embrace with the moment. It was loud, it was awe-inspiring, and it was all ours.

The crowd was erupting. I looked over at Brian Pitt, the band's drummer; sweat was cascading down his face. We exchanged a glance before Robbie West, the late-eighties megastar, acknowledged the musicians over the microphone. Take a bow, feel good, life gets no better. This was always a great moment in a show; you'd given your all, all energy was spent.

It was also, by design, a long way from the world I used to know.

I looked around, soaking in the atmosphere a little more. The Hollywood Bowl was a stunning place to play. It had history and a story to tell. Standing on that stage, in the footprints of the Beatles and the Doors, was surreal. As we moved offstage toward the stairs to our VIP band room, I felt fortunate I had found refuge in this eccentric and chaotic industry.

Outsiders often think it must be glamorous and exciting backstage at a big show. It's not. The mood is hectic, road crews and techs are moving gear everywhere, and you're always stepping out of someone's way. Musicians stand around either patting each other on the back for a great show performed or getting themselves in the zone for a great show about to be performed. Lead singers are usually just standing around patting themselves on the back.

Among the chaos, the first person I saw was Greatrex.

"Great show," he said.

"Yeah," I was still catching my breath.

Greatrex had been with me forever. He was my keyboard tech and closest friend. Once, we had been brothers-in-arms, literally. Jack Greatrex. There wasn't a soul I trusted more in this world. The stage lights cast shadows over his perspiring face. People often judged him based on his shaved head, goatee and large frame. You just had to look a little harder to see the passion and intelligence behind those piercing blue eyes. We had each other's backs, we read each other's thoughts. It had always been that way.

My immediate agenda involved a cool shower, a change of clothes, and an ice-cold beer. The sweat was starting to close in around me, revival was the order of the day. Robbie, our singer, had his own dressing room; after all, he was the star and we were his hired hands, so most of the publicists and record company "hangers on" were waiting for him there. In our room were those who I regarded as the more genuine part of the music industry: fellow musicians, girlfriends, friends, and occasionally some very attractive friends of friends. What can I say? It comes with the job.

"Nicholas Sharp," I heard my name coming from the doorway. It was Dave, the lead singer with the headlining band. Famous human.

"Great freaking playing man. Next time we're in the studio, come and have a play."

I was a little stunned, but in a good way.

"Thanks so much, Dave. You bet I'll be there."

"Cool, see ya."

Dave moved on to get ready for his show. He was a hero of mine. One of the nice parts of this industry was meeting heroes. I once shook Paul McCartney's hand. A Beatle. If by any remote chance I should go to heaven when I die, I reckon God would have a hard time topping that one.

In the nineties, Dave had been in a very successful grunge band that had taken the world by storm. It had all ended when their lead singer died a tragically early death. Music can be a tough business. It's a mix of vulnerability and toughness not needed in many other lines of work. After a time, however, Dave had bounced back and now led his own world-beating band. Just the fact he knew my name was cool enough, but to be invited onto a session with his band was something else.

As I walked into our band room, there were a few good-natured jibes from my friends and colleagues—"Who's gonna be a star?" etc. I didn't want to be a star; I just wanted to be the best musician I could be.

The conversation was warm, the beer was cold, and the room was just starting to thin out when behind me I heard the familiar voice of Greatrex. He had just finished his keyboard tech duties upstairs.

"Nick, I only just checked for messages. There was a call for you." I always gave Greatrex my phone when I was onstage.

"It was Leyla, and Nick, she said it was urgent, and she

3

sounded worried."

I moved over to Greatrex so no one else could hear our conversation. "How worried?"

"Worried," he said.

Suddenly, I felt cold. Leyla didn't scare easily. "Did you call her back?" I asked.

"I tried, but there was no answer."

"Pass me the phone, I'll try now." Greatrex did as requested. I listened to Leyla's message and then tried the number. I tried it again. A foreboding gloom was coming over me; I told myself not to overreact. The problem was, however, that I had spent my whole life trusting my instincts, and my life had been spared several times because I had.

"Let's go," I motioned to Greatrex, but he was already packing up our bags. We said our goodbyes and moved out of the room. I couldn't help but think we got a couple of strange looks as we left, or maybe it was me who had the strange look.

Unpredictable circumstances. Suddenly, five years ago felt like yesterday.

Greatrex and I made our way down through the bowels of the stadium. When we reached the VIP exit, we had to wait for the luxury shuttle bus to take us back to the hotel that was our meeting place before the concert. I had left my car there; this was LA, my hometown. In LA, your car was everything. Neither Greatrex nor I said a word, each in our own world.

It wasn't until we were purring up the road in my stylishly unfashionable retro XJS Jaguar that we started to talk.

"It's probably nothing," said Greatrex.

"Do you believe that?" I asked.

"No."

We both knew something was likely wrong. Leyla had not

lived the life she had by calling out for help every time some minor problem got in her way. Greatrex nodded. Honesty had always been strong between us, especially in times of stress, and we had shared too many of those.

We didn't say another word as the pull of the Jaguar's V12 engine launched us along the US-101. Perhaps to distract myself, I began to reflect on Leyla, and the events of the last few years. This was something I tried to avoid. I'm usually good at avoidance, but not today.

Just like the car we were traveling in, I seemed to be a conflicted mess of European style and the need for American muscle and power. My mother was English, a concert pianist of some note. My bent for music and performing had come from her. My father was the exact opposite; an American colonel in the United States Marines, he was a man of order, discipline, and regiment. Both my parents had instilled in me a sense of purpose and morality; it's something they both had in bucketloads, though expressed in different ways. I had followed my father's line of work. As it turned out, that had been a mistake.

"Turnoff coming up," said Greatrex, jolting me from my way too self-indulgent thoughts.

We headed west down the 405. I turned up the music on the car stereo to keep me from thinking bad things; it didn't work. We veered off the 405 through a series of turns until we came left onto North Venice Boulevard, by the water. I could see the Santa Monica Pier and the fun park ahead as we drove toward Venice Beach and its permanent carnival atmosphere. After too many years as a Marine Scout Sniper sitting alone on hilltops and rooftops, it suited me to be around people.

I lived in an old stucco building in an upstairs apartment

overlooking the Pacific Ocean. It was not luxurious, but it was comfortable. I opened the front door. My gleaming black Yamaha grand piano sat in the corner of the lounge by the window, awaiting my next music-therapy session. Right now, I was more focused on the telephone answering service than exorcizing demons. I needed to hear Leyla's voice telling me everything was alright, I needed to speak to her, and I needed to know she was safe. I listened for messages. There was just a repeat of Leyla's message on my cell: "Nick, call me, it's urgent." It turned out I got nothing I needed.

I looked at Greatrex; he had the same tense look on his face that I felt on mine.

"What now?" he asked.

"I go," I responded.

"We go."

"No, I go alone. I need you here in case Leyla makes contact or sends a message. Besides, we have commitments in the recording studio in two days' time. Wayne will have a fit if we don't turn up or both disappear off the map."

Wayne De Soto was my extremely hardworking manager. He had put a lot of work into my new career and I didn't want to disappoint him.

"I need you to prepare the equipment for that. Hopefully, I'll sort out whatever the issue is and be back well before session time."

As it turned out, I'd never been more wrong in my life.

# Chapter 2

Again, the loud roar, but this time it was a jet engine. I was on board an Alaska Airlines 737 hurtling down the runway at LAX. I spent most of the trip regretting I'd not come here direct from the concert. It would have saved precious time. It was only three hours since the end of the show at the Bowl, but I felt a world away.

As the plane sped into the night sky, I had no way of knowing the impact of the journey that lay ahead of me. Ignorance is bliss.

It was a ninety-minute flight through the evening to Portland, Oregon, where Leyla now lived. The night lights of LA seemed to take forever to pass over. Everything seemed so calm and leisurely onboard the plane, but I was the opposite. I was restless, agitated, and uncertain of what lay ahead. Leyla used to joke that I was always so calm in an emergency while others around me became excited. The flip side was right here: while others around me were calm, I was bouncing out of my brain with impatience.

As the aircraft soared through the night, I once again found myself lost in reflection.

Leyla Salib had lived her whole life in Iraq, until a few short years ago. She and her beautiful three-year-old daughter,

Amira, had lived on the outskirts of Baghdad with Leyla's husband, Akram. In war-torn Iraq, money was hard to come by, and life was difficult. Akram had a young family to take care of, so like any responsible parent he looked for alternative forms of income.

In time, he began work as a translator for the coalition forces. Akram was good at what he did, and after a few months the powers that be realized he was not only a gifted translator but also in a position to provide information that helped them plan successful strategies against the insurgents. Akram had access to areas and communities that no regular intelligence officer could enter. People were not afraid to talk in front of him as they would be in front of an outsider.

As Akram's value as an asset increased in his minder's eyes, the information he provided became more and more important. Throughout this period, Akram was providing well for his young family.

After a while, however, things started to go wrong. People in positions of power started noticing that the information Akram was providing was not yielding the same positive results; in fact, at times it seemed downright unreliable.

Everything came to a head one balmy Iraqi evening when a small task force of Marine special forces was sent in to take down an insurgent leader. The information that Akram had provided turned out to be wrong, very wrong. Three of the special forces men were killed in an ambush that night, and the others barely made it out alive.

Rumors spread that Akram had now turned, and that he was an insurgent double agent.

At that point Akram became an enemy of the coalition. In a dark, off-the-books operation, ordered and sanctioned only by one man in the intelligence division, Akram was dealt with, permanently. His life ended in a dark alleyway as he walked home from a community meeting. Akram would never see or hold his wife and child again.

Though this was a frustratingly sad story for the families of all involved, in the relentless battle for the freedom and hearts the Iraqi people, anguish and tragedy were not unusual. What happened next, however, was very, very unusual.

In time, more information came to light. It appeared it was not Akram's information that was incorrect but rather the spin that was put on it by his controlling officer, Major Giles Winter. Although it was never officially proven, it was suspected that Winter was working to his own agenda, an agenda that pursued personal financial profit over the interests of the coalition forces and the Iraqi people.

Of course, with not enough proof at hand that would stack up in a military court, the whole situation was quietly swept under the carpet and forgotten. Major Winter was shipped back stateside, left the military, and eventually disappeared. It never came to light that Akram's assassination was a rogue action authorized by Winter alone. Accordingly, no overtly official attempt was made to give support to Akram's young wife, Leyla, or his daughter, Amira.

At the time, I was posted at Camp Striker, part of the Victory Base Complex in Baghdad. It took a while for the facts to dribble down to my team. It took me even longer to realize the full role Winter had played in the situation. Although we felt bad about it, there was nothing that could be done without official cooperation.

It was then that we received information that the local insurgent leaders had decided that Akram Salib's family should be made an example of, to ensure no more locals would work with the coalition. A kill order was put out on Leyla and Amira Salib.

When a group of us learned this, we decided we could not stand by and let it happen. We went to our commanding officer, Colonel Colin Devlin-Waters. Although he met with us, Devlin-Waters let us know his hands were officially tied. With no legal evidence proving otherwise, Akram was still officially a traitor who worked for the insurgency. Though everyone in the room knew this to be false, those in a position of enough power to do something about it were unable to act.

Time was our biggest issue; we didn't know when the insurgent strike team was going to hit the young family. Between us, our team, including Jack Greatrex and myself, had enough contacts in the transport division to get Leyla and Amira a seat on a military transport out of there. The trouble was, without the right paperwork they weren't going anywhere.

The next evening, after the failed meeting with our commanding officer, I arrived back at my barracks to find an envelope on my bunk. Opening it, I found passports and US travel papers for Leyla and Amira. With the papers was a note with one word scrawled: "deniable." I suspected that our Colonel Devlin-Waters had pulled some unofficial strings and managed to arrange the papers. I had no doubt they were to some extent forged, but they would suffice to get the girls out. We should, however, expect no more help from our leaders.

The rest was pretty straightforward, a midnight visit to Leyla's home not only to collect the girls, but also to persuade them that they were in danger and had to leave. Our argument was helped when the insurgent strike team turned up around fifteen minutes after we arrived. A brief firefight ensued, and our well-trained team got the better of the insurgents.

After a short trip to the coalition-held airport in the back of an informally seconded military truck, and being given two seats on a late-night military flight to the US, the girls were ready to go.

Just before Greatrex and I put Leyla and Amira on that plane, Leyla turned to me with a questioning look. "Why are you doing this for us?" Both Greatrex and the girls looked at me expectantly, though he already knew my answer.

Memory is a strange thing; sometimes you forget experiences that you wanted to remember, and some things you'd rather let go stay with you forever. This was a case of the latter. Sitting in the protected comfort of my seat, flying through the night to Portland, I recalled every sound, every smell, every emotion that ran through me in that long moment on the tarmac on that humid Iraqi evening.

I remembered clearly the trust and belief emanating from Leyla's and Amira's frightened eyes. I recalled myself trembling in frustration as I wanted to say something to make things right but found no words. I'd just quietly guided those two shaken souls silently onto the transport plane.

I'd known clearly why I was doing what I was doing, and it was knowledge that would haunt me forever. I was the sniper in that alleyway in suburban Baghdad. I had been sent out there by Giles Winter. I had pulled the trigger. I had murdered Leyla's husband.

# Chapter 3

I awoke to screeching tires as the plane touched down on the tarmac in Portland. I must have dozed off. It was now time to move quickly. The combined international and domestic airport in Portland is not large by American standards, and I had no luggage to collect, so I moved quickly through the terminal to collect my rental car.

I headed south on the 205. I had been to Portland several times to check in on Leyla and Amira over the last few years. I felt like her overprotective older brother. Leyla had wanted to live in Portland because she had heard that it rained a lot there. It didn't rain much in Iraq, and she had wanted to get as far away as possible from her memories.

I understood and had arranged a small house for the two of them in a quiet suburb not far from the beach. I hadn't mentioned at the time that I was quietly pleased with Leyla's choice of location because it was close enough to LA that I could be there quickly if something went wrong. It appeared something had gone wrong.

I drove quickly. No one pulled me over, no one slowed me down, I made good time. Around thirty minutes after leaving the airport, I turned into Leyla's street. I didn't know what to expect. I had tried her on my cell phone several times on the way over, there was still no answer. My unease increased as I turned into her driveway.

What I saw before me was something I was certainly not expecting. Leyla's Toyota was in the driveway, and there were lights on in the house. Through the drapes I could see two people moving around in the lounge room, and their silhouettes looked remarkably like Leyla and Amira. As I got out of the car, I heard their television. I relaxed a little. It was looking as though this may have been a big misunderstanding, a lack of communication, and hopefully a needless trip.

I virtually leaped up the pathway and knocked on the door. To my relief, Leyla opened the door. I could feel the smile widening on my face as she led me into her small lounge room.

The time it takes to react to a dangerous situation is considerably longer from a relaxed state of mind than an alert one. Just ask any soldier who's been on patrol in or near enemy-held territory. For this reason, it became apparent that my relief was not only premature but also part of someone else's plan.

In my excitement I hadn't noticed the stress in Leyla's welcoming smile or the stiffness with which she moved. I noticed it now; it was pointed out to me clearly by the sharp pain inflicted by a gun barrel shoved in my back. Any uncertainty was removed by a male voice with an overly negative vocabulary saying, "No movement, no reaching into pockets, no talk."

Looking across the small lounge room, the first thing I saw was Amira, her sleek dark hair cut in a new, fashionable bob style. She was in the far corner playing with a doll. I recognized the doll; I had given it to her for her last birthday. Leyla had moved to the couch on the far wall and was sitting down. She looked a bundle of nerves. On the positive side, both Leyla and Amira appeared to be unharmed.

"I am so sorry, Nick," she said. "They came out of nowhere and surprised us in the mall car park."

There was a lack of certainty, a frailty in her usually self-assured voice.

"Don't worry, Leyla," I said. "We'll—"

My sentence was stopped short by an agonizing pain in the back of my head. The man behind me had pistol-whipped me. Through my light-headedness I saw Leyla grimace, and I heard Amira's piercing scream.

"Uncle Nick," she cried out.

"I said no talk. For a musician, you don't hear so good," said my attacker. More of a sarcastic chuckle, really.

I could feel adrenaline flowing through my body. I had felt pain such as this before. I knew it would eventually recede, but the horror displayed in that little girl's voice would stay with her for a very long time. I started to speak again but realized that would only cause more pain for me and more stress for Amira and Leyla, so I bit my tongue.

It seemed like an age, though it was probably only a few seconds before anyone spoke. During this time, I recovered quickly, and a plan started to form in my mind. I always like to have a plan.

I put the musician in me to one side, perhaps a little too easily. As a Marine, I had been trained in hand-to-hand combat, and the man behind me had made a mistake. If you are going to cover another person with a gun, it should be done from at least four feet way, or your prisoner can pivot and sweep the gun from your hand before you have realized what was happening.

I had a plan, then I didn't.

There had been no mistake. Another man, around six-foot-four and built like the proverbial barn, came from the kitchen. His gun was around eight feet away and pointed directly at me. This guy had me totally covered. I would have more chance of singing my way out of the situation than using hand-to-hand techniques. I didn't sing.

"Nicholas Sharp." The second man had a voice, and it was no friendlier than the first. "Sit down on the couch next to your lady friend. I think you would be less dangerous if you were sitting down."

I didn't feel very dangerous, but there was no point in arguing. I sat down next to Leyla. Amira had run over to her when I was hit, and the little girl would not let go of her mother's arm.

"We will keep this simple and brief." The second man was definitely the alpha here.

"Is that because you don't know any long words?" I said.

I wanted to destress the situation for Amira's sake. Also, humor helped me convince myself I was not worried when the reality was the opposite.

The first man started to raise the butt of his pistol and move toward me.

"No," cried Leyla and Amira simultaneously.

"No," said the bigger intruder. "No more violence unless absolutely necessary."

"There you go," I said, turning to my potential assailant. "The no's have it." I winked at Amira. She almost smiled.

If looks could kill, the man behind me would have no trouble staring down a nuclear bomb. I wasn't making any new friends.

15

"Mr. Sharp." Number two again; number one seemed to have lost his will to speak. "You will shortly be asked to perform a series of small tasks. What you will be asked to do will be relatively simple but with some risk, though only to yourself. We needed to set up this meeting to make sure we would have your complete attention and to ensure your total cooperation."

I started to interrupt but again thought the better of it; the first man was ready to boil over.

"In the meantime," continued the second man, "you are to carry on your activities as normal, including fulfilling all your musical commitments, until you hear from us. We will know if you deviate from your normal routine, and there will be consequences. For the moment, these two ladies will be our guests at a location of our choosing. Basically, from this point on, you work for us." The man's smile conveyed purely evil intent.

I didn't believe for a second that I was the only one experiencing risk here, and although worried as all hell, I then asked the stupidest of stupid questions.

"Why do you need to take Leyla and Amira?"

"It is an old cliché, Mr. Sharp, but you are a musician now; you should be used to clichés. We need these ladies to ensure that you will do exactly as we ask, when we ask, and do it without alerting any authorities. Is that clear?"

"Like crystal," I responded, this time no joke.

As I spoke, the front door opened and another man, probably even bigger than the first two, walked in the room.

"I've disconnected and removed some essential parts of Sharp's car engine. He will not be following us."

My dad, the late Colonel Brighton Sharp, had a saying he'd

always lived by when it came to any sort of conflict: "never let them know you're scared." It appeared to have rubbed off on me.

"The three of you," I observed, my mouth starting to go into gear without requesting permission from my brain, "you don't seem the types to have the intellectual prowess to roll with this. Who's really behind this sick little plan?"

From there, all I remember is pain and darkness. It must have just got too much for my number one friend with the pistol butt.

# Chapter 4

"Where to next?"

The early afternoon Californian sun was warm, and the Heineken in front of me was ice cold. The Pacific was a glistening mass of blue, an endless and surrounding seascape. I looked across the water and took in views from Malibu in the north, down the coast to South Bay.

It was the afternoon of the day after my failed rescue bid in Portland. Jack Greatrex and I were sitting at our preferred table at the Mariasol Cocina Mexicana at the ocean end of the Santa Monica Pier. He was waiting for an answer to a question that I hadn't even heard.

My mind was going over and over the events of the last twenty-four hours and the seemingly growing list of stupid mistakes I had made.

I had regained consciousness around twenty minutes after being knocked out by the thug at Leyla's house. I spent the next fifteen minutes trying to get my brain to function with some sort of normality. In movies, people get hit in the head all the time and just seem to bounce back straight away. No one ever mentions the lingering effects of concussion. I'd been hit twice, and my brain just didn't seem to want to play ball with my intentions.

I eventually got myself sorted out and then spent an hour combing Leyla and Amira's home for any sign of who their abductors may be, or where they had taken them. There was, of course, no sign, no clue, nothing.

It then took a wait of thirty minutes for a cab to arrive and take me to the airport. During this time, I phoned the rental car company and told them I'd had a breakdown and my car needed to be picked up. I didn't tell them the circumstances. The one thing I remembered clearly was the instruction not to call the authorities, and I didn't want the rental company alerting them either.

In the cab on the way to catch a plane home, I phoned Greatrex. He picked up on the first ring. I told him briefly and quietly of the events of the previous couple of hours.

It was on the flight back that I really began to beat myself up. Why hadn't I played for longer to try to find out more information instead of making wiseass cracks to the abductors and provoking them? Why had I gone to Leyla's house alone? If Greatrex had been there we would have been some sort of match for those idiots. But, of course, those thugs were not idiots; they were professionals who had set me up, and I'd acted exactly as they had expected. Who was the idiot now?

By the time I'd arrived home I'd been exhausted, and after filling Greatrex in with a few more details I'd gone straight to sleep. It was relief, even if only temporary.

Greatrex had stayed over. He'd had enough medical training to know that in cases of concussion the first twenty-four hours are vital, and the patient needed to be monitored. Of course, I had refused to seek any more formal medical attention. That would involve too many questions.

In the morning we decided to test the waters and check out if we really were being watched, or if it was a bluff. I drove down to the Santa Monica Police Department just off the freeway and pulled the Jag up directly out front. I sat there for about twenty seconds before my cell rang. It was a text message, a one-word warning: "mistake."

We were being watched and warned. I drove off.

Greatrex and I had then wandered the length of the Santa Monica Pier trying to spot any tail behind us. We didn't see anyone.

We were regular customers at the restaurant and had enjoyed many meals there, but on this day we had little appetite. The location, however, enabled us to keep our surroundings under careful view.

We poked at our food. Even the cold beer did little to improve our state of mind. It certainly didn't numb the fear we felt for the girls' safety.

"Where to next?" Greatrex repeated his earlier question.

"I just don't know." It was not the response he was hoping for. Nicholas Sharp, man of indecision.

"We need to plan. We always used to have a plan," said my friend.

"The trouble is, back in the day, we were the ones instigating action; now we're the ones responding to it." We were in unfamiliar territory here.

I watched a thirty-foot sailboat glide past in the distance, seemingly without a care in the world. I was jealous. I loved sailing. I loved the idea of not having a care in the world. I sighed.

"From what you've told me, we know these people are professionals," said Greatrex.

"But what we don't know is what they want," I continued. "I

think we can assume that it's me or us that they are after, and that Leyla and Amira are hopefully just a sideshow, temporary collateral damage."

"The real worry is that if you do what they want, will they release the girls?"

There you go; Greatrex had said it out loud, the great fear that was clearly at the forefront of both our minds. It only felt worse hearing him say it.

"What I don't get is who would want a retired Marine sniper turned musician to do anything. There are plenty of people out there who are current, not rusty like me. There are also plenty who are willing to take on a contract for cash. More to the point, most of those people have not turned away from the assassination business with a clearly stated lack of willingness to ever kill on order again." It made sense as I said it.

Greatrex took a sip of his beer.

"What if …" Greatrex paused, but he had my attention. "What if it was the combination of your music and military skills these people were chasing?"

It seemed far-fetched to me, but we had nothing else.

The last thing in the world I wanted was to be drawn back into the past … Correction, second last thing. The last thing I wanted was for Leyla and Amira to be harmed.

"We can talk until the sun goes down," I said, "but at the end of the day we won't know anything until they contact us. We can only assume and hope that the girls are all right and that these people need them to keep us in line. In the meantime, as difficult as it is, we must carry on as normal."

I paid our bill and we headed back down the pier toward home. Between the fear and the anticipation, I couldn't help but feel we were going to know a lot more very soon. Perhaps it was better not knowing.

# Chapter 5

Three hours out of LA, in the middle of the Mojave Desert, inspired by the vast desert environment in which it sits, the Rancho de la Luna recording studio is worlds away from the city's madness. Greatrex and I stared silently ahead as we drove there through the sun-soaked desert.

We were surrounded by almost endless space, scattered Joshua trees and 140 miles of darkest thought. Someone once said that to appreciate this kind of country, the "desert needs to be in you." The desert certainly influenced a lot of musicians through the years. This is probably why Rancho de la Luna existed. I was a sea and saltwater kind of guy, but I was in awe of this vast landscape. It also suited my bleak mood.

I was booked for a session there with an aging progressive rock band trying to rediscover their magic and capitalize on the current retro music revival. I had no choice but to keep the date.

It had been two days since my visit to Leyla's house, and we had heard nothing. Knowing we were being watched, we had been careful about making some discreet inquiries about the three men who had taken the girls. Nothing but dead ends. We were tired, we were angry, and as each hour went by, we were growing more and more frustrated.

Greatrex was driving. His SUV allowed us to sit high enough above the road so that we had a clear view all around us, or so we thought.

Out of nowhere, a loud motor thundered above us.

"Probably sightseers," said Greatrex, as the chopper fled into the distance.

"It was pretty low," I responded. "You would think any tourist would be freaked out traveling at that height."

Before Greatrex could respond, the chopper turned in the distance. We could only just make it out in the glare of the desert sun, but it seemed to be coming back toward us. It was flying low, very low.

"Watch out," I yelled. They were wasted words, as Greatrex was already pumping the breaks and swerving to avoid the flying machine in front of us. The chopper landed about ten feet in front of where our car had stopped. It was like a dark mechanical ghost, jet-black with no markings. The windows were also tinted black. We could not see inside.

"Not liking this," said Greatrex, as he reached into his glove box for his old Glock 19 service revolver. At this point I was kind of glad he'd hung onto it from the old days.

"I'm with you, but I don't see a lot of choices in front of us right now. Keep the gun close but play it cool." Greatrex was born cool. He also reached down and pulled a couple of small black boxes out of a side compartment and slipped them into his pocket. I recognized them as electronic trackers. Greatrex always thought ahead of the game.

In front of us, the chopper door opened. I wasn't surprised when two of my new best friends from Portland got out. It would have been a fairly even match if they weren't each pointing an AK-47 machine gun directly at us.

"Never liked those things," said Greatrex, "inaccurate and messy."

I didn't want to be part of the mess.

"Out, hands behind your head," ordered the first man that I had met in Portland. He looked as though he expected to be obeyed.

We got out of the car.

"I believe you were instructed to put your hands behind your heads." These words came from a different voice, the source as yet out of sight, behind the helicopter. The cold, lifeless, arrogant tone continued, "It's not a day to be rebellious, Nicholas Sharp, that is ... if you want to see your lady friend ... and her daughter again."

I felt myself go rigid as the recognition dawned on me. This was not going to go well.

A tall, tanned, all too familiar figure with dark hair and darker eyes appeared from the other side of the helicopter.

He smiled, I shuddered.

I would rather have faced off with the devil than the creature who stood in front of me.

"Giles Winter." I choked on the words as I spat them out. There was probably a lot I wanted to say, and even more I needed to say, but as I stared at the bastard who had sent me to assassinate Leyla's husband, Akram Salib, all those years ago, all I could do was implode with rage.

"Easy," said Greatrex in a quiet voice. "There's a lot at stake here." He sounded to me like he was fighting his own war of control in the depths of his soul.

"You appear to be a little lost for words, Sharp. I thought you would have more to say when we caught up with each other again." Winter's voice was smug and emotionless, the voice of a sociopath.

I felt myself regaining some self-control. I had to now accept that a drive through the desert had just become a descent into hell.

"Let's begin with a chat about old times, shall we?"

I chose not to respond.

"I never had the opportunity to express my gratitude for the work you did for me in Iraq. Back then, things were starting to get a bit difficult for a man in my … er … position. That Iraqi fellow, what was his name? Ah yes, Salib, well, he was getting just a bit too close to some facts I wanted to remain undetected, particularly regarding those people who were making my efforts so "worthwhile," shall we say. Unfortunately, he had to be permanently removed from the scene."

The sneer on Giles Winter's face as he uttered those words made it clear "remorse" was not a term he understood.

He continued, "I knew that the Marines' top Scout Sniper, the legendary Nicholas Sharp, was just the man for the job. That's why I brought you in. You did what I needed done. You followed orders. That's what you people do, isn't it? Blindly follow orders. No matter what the consequence. Of course, I owe you my thanks."

Like all sociopaths, Giles Winter loved the sound of his own voice and seemed genuinely amused by his own cleverness.

Finally, I found some words of my own. "There is not a word in any language that would describe you, Winter. You are beyond the darkest side of humanity. You sold out your country, you arranged to set up and slaughter an innocent man, and now you threaten the life of his family." As I spoke, I felt my voice quiver and my rage grow. I also felt Greatrex's hand on my arm.

"Bring it down, bring it down," he whispered.

He was right; losing it now would achieve nothing for Leyla and Amira, and I was close to losing it.

"Actually, there *is* a word to describe me." Satan had spoken again. "Successful."

Nicholas Sharp, man of language: no response, just a cold, intense hatred.

Jack Greatrex spoke across the space between the two of us and Winter for the first time. "Clearly, you have the advantage here, Winter. You already know what you want us to do. We have no idea. You have the girls. We don't know where they are. Cut out the Bond villain speeches and tell us what you want."

Jack Greatrex, a man who gets to the point.

"Santori." As Winter spoke, he looked at the first man from Portland. "Please guide Mr. Sharp and Mr. Greatrex down the embankment so we can go for a stroll. There is no point in risking undue attention, even on this lonely road. Rowley, follow behind."

Now both the Portland enforcers had names. As we walked off, the helicopter powered up and took off. I assumed it was likely piloted by the third man I had met in Portland.

"Don't worry, Mr. Sharp. He will be back to pick us up."

That's not what I was worrying about. When a bad man asks you to take a walk through the desert, nothing good usually comes of it. Greatrex and I looked at each other, both feeling pretty helpless. The pointy end of an AK-47 a few feet from your back will do that.

"They won't harm us while they need us," I whispered. Again, I was finding myself reluctantly shutting out the musician and letting Marine Sharp back in. Necessity breeds what it breeds.

"A great theory, here's hoping," Greatrex replied.

We walked on silently for around ten minutes in that same formation, Santori in the lead, Greatrex and I following. Winter to one side and Rowley behind us. These people were professionals.

The sun was hot, the land was dry and rocky. I was concentrating on the vain hope that a rattlesnake would appear from behind a rock and bite Winter. I should have known; rattlesnakes don't bite their own kind.

"Enough," I heard a voice say. To my surprise, it was mine. "We are not taking another step until you explain exactly what's going on, Winter."

The butt of an AK-47 caused an explosion of pain in the back of my head.

Greatrex balled his fists.

"We'll let you know when it is enough," said Santori. Just a little reminder of who was in charge.

Just to underscore the point, Giles Winter walked around six more paces and then commanded, "Stop here." He turned to me.

"Now, Sharp, if you are done with your pointless protests, we need to have a chat. You and Mr. Greatrex need to listen very carefully. If you follow my instructions, there is a good chance the two of you will survive, along with your friends from Iraq. If you don't, I can personally offer a prolonged and painful death to all four of you."

Giles Winter certainly knew how to get our attention.

"In three weeks, you two are leaving on a tour of US army bases in Iraq, supporting your eighties has-been singer friend, Robbie West. You will be in Iraq for several days and then return via England, where you are performing at the Isle of

Wight Festival."

"What makes you think that?" I responded. The festival gig was well publicized, but the visit to Iraq was secret. It had to be that way for the safety of the entertainers. "I think you are imagining things, Winter."

"Please don't insult me, Sharp. I belong to a well-connected network. I knew about your Iraq tour before you did."

Greatrex and I glanced at each other. Giles Winter certainly appeared very well connected, and his connections appeared to run deep into the US military.

He continued, "I have some materials in Iraq that I need shipped back to the United States. The materials I speak of are extremely … ah … sensitive. I cannot bring them back through normal means."

Winter was sounding very confident.

"This is where your efforts will be required. You will bring back a package concealed in your musical equipment. Of course, your equipment won't be searched, as it is permanently under watch within the military machine." Winter smiled his cold smile. "Simple, isn't it? You do what I ask, I see no reason for you not to live."

Senses working overtime. I smelled a rat. A big, murderous, deceptive rat.

"You've gone to an awful lot of trouble to set this up, Winter. You've taken Leyla and Amira; you're extorting us. There are a thousand ways to smuggle items back from Iraq now that the main conflict is well and truly over. I just don't buy it." Nicholas Sharp, extremely clever man.

"Mildly perceptive, Sharp. Allow me to explain."

Winter sat on a log and made himself comfortable. I knew he must be feeling the effect of the sun as much as we were, but I figured he had the advantage of ice flowing through his veins.

"If you remember back several years, the main reason the coalition forces went into Iraq after 9/11 was because they believed Saddam Hussein had a stockpile of chemical weapons and was prepared to use them."

"That myth was blown wide open," Greatrex intervened. "When no chemical weapons were found, the public and press held the coalition leaders accountable. This is all on the public record."

"Yes, they did," said Winter, "and it is well documented. In fact, my colleagues throughout our network spent a great deal of time and money making sure that happened. Well-placed leaks, funds exchanging hands, et cetera. It was quite an effort over a considerable period, in fact a much longer period than you might imagine."

I didn't like where this was going. Winter got up and began to pace.

"What people don't know, except for an informed few, is that Saddam Hussein did have chemical weapons, very powerful and effective weapons. Without the hindrance of regulations and oversight, his regime was able to produce possibly the most powerful chemical weapons and nerve agents ever created." Winter produced a smile that sent a shiver down to my core.

"Our people were made aware of these weapons well before the coalition invasion," he said. "We not only knew about them, we also knew where they were. Saddam's one disadvantage was that he hadn't yet refined a way to effectively release and deliver the weapons. Accordingly, he couldn't use them en masse against the coalition forces. He knew this, we knew this.

It was obvious his regime was going to fail, so we made him an offer too good to refuse."

I felt a cloak of darkness falling over me.

Winter went on. "We arranged for most of the chemical stocks to be destroyed, but samples of the weapons were to be held in a safe location known only to my people. Reverse engineering is an amazing craft. We would be able to reproduce as much of the Iraqi chemical weaponry as we needed. The plan was that in exchange for the weapons samples and formulas, we would help Saddam escape Iraq and avoid capture."

"But he didn't escape; he was captured by coalition forces." Nicholas Sharp stating the obvious, again.

"Very true, Mr. Sharp." Winter was hitting his stride now. "It also took quite a bit of arranging to make that happen. In the end, it didn't suit us for him to walk free. It was, of course, no coincidence that I was assigned to duty in Baghdad. While ostensibly working in intelligence for the coalition forces, my real role was to keep an eye on our small stockpile of sample weapons for our network and to ensure Saddam Hussein's capture. I was also responsible for making sure the coalition never knew what we were up to. What better place to do it than from the coalition intelligence service?"

Again, the smile of the devil.

"Of course, as I mentioned, your friend's husband, Mr. Salib, got wind of what was going on, hence our need to access your particular talents."

I wanted to leap forward and grab Winter around the throat, but the memory of the AK-47 butt was still reverberating through my skull. I did nothing.

"Now we come to our current situation." Winter was really

enjoying this. "Unfortunately, our supply line out of Iraq was recently discovered by the coalition. We were able to explain it off as a Turkish smuggler's operation, but its discovery did leave us without a workable route out of Iraq for our weapon samples and formulas. Imagine my joy, Nicholas Sharp, when I learned that you had left the forces and become a successful working musician, of all things, especially one with a clearance to tour military bases. Once again, you were in a position to help our network with our plans."

"I won't do it," I said.

Santori gave me a provocative look that promised more violence, but Winter dismissed him with a glance.

"Oh, you will do it, Mr. Sharp. You self-righteous, mightier-than-thou types always do, especially if you think you are saving lives. And make no mistake, Mr. Sharp, you are saving lives: those of your Leyla and Amira, and your own."

Winter looked me straight in the eye. He was sounding more condescending than ever.

"And … er … by the way. If you or Mr. Greatrex should think of sacrificing your two Iraqi friends for the sake of some greater good, think again. Information has been arranged to surface regarding both of you and your involvement in the assassination of Akram Salib. This information provides provable facts that suggest both you and Mr. Greatrex were working solely to further your own financial interests. Just to make doubly sure, monies have also been deposited in both your bank accounts relating to this and other actions. Even if you went to the authorities, they would not believe the story of two people with such blemished records." Winter smiled. "Again, let's be clear about this, Mr. Sharp—you will do exactly as I say."

# Chapter 6

The walk back to the road, still in the same rigid formation, seemed to happen in slow motion. I was trying to come to terms with too many things at once. My thoughts were racing. Leyla and Amira were in danger, and it seemed they were going to stay that way for a while.

My recent life as a musician, my refuge, had just been blown apart, and the past was clawing at me, drawing me back. I didn't want to go. It also looked like Greatrex and I were about to become responsible for smuggling high-grade chemical weapons into the United States. It was all way too much to process. I felt an empty feeling in the pit of my stomach as I realized I could see no alternative, no way out.

The big fella, Greatrex, was on the ball before me.

"I have an idea," he whispered, glancing down at his pocket with the pistol in it. In their overconfident zeal, our hosts hadn't searched us. AK-47s trump all.

"I'm listening," I said quietly.

"I have a little extra something."

"A little something. Okay, do what you need to do. I'll try create a distraction," I responded. "But one thing," I whispered.

Greatrex looked at me quizzically.

"The girls. We have to be playing the long game here, just

doing some damage and getting out now is not enough."

Greatrex now looked at me as though I was a poor student who couldn't grasp a concept. Nicholas Sharp, simple-minded.

"The long game," he repeated.

As we climbed the embankment back to the road, where the chopper was now waiting, I pretended to stumble. It was an old trick, but it worked. Behind me Rowley reacted with speed by moving forward and pressing the barrel of his gun hard against my back. At last, a mistake. As I went down, I grabbed the gun and, using my feet as leverage, flipped him over me and onto the road next to the big black machine. There was a risk of Rowley firing, but I didn't think he would.

At the same time, Greatrex had pushed into Santori's shoulder, shoving him hard into the side of the chopper. Santori recovered quickly, sending Greatrex to the ground with a swift kick, expertly administered. Rowley had also rallied speedily, as I expected him to. He was looking at me, pointing his gun at me with anticipation, as though I was the major threat in his immediate world. I expected him to do this as well; I did nothing except look up at him.

Greatrex was climbing to his feet, using both hands to steady himself against the helicopter. It was over before it began.

"One more pathetic move like that and one of the Iraqi girls will die tonight." Giles Winter's tone left no doubt as to his intention. "That will still leave one alive, with her future precariously placed in your hands, Mr. Sharp and Mr. Greatrex. You will not impede our plans with stupid macho demonstrations such as this."

Again, he looked directly at me. "I would have thought better of you, Sharp."

Winter and his men were firmly back in control now. I had

to talk, say something, keep Winter's attention on me.

"You may be the one calling the shots for now, Winter, but that won't last forever." Yet again, the rifle butt, this time in the solar plexus. The pain was excruciating.

"Enough. Santori, Rowley, into the helicopter." The henchmen moved toward the machine while keeping their guns trained on us.

At the last minute, Winter stopped. He seemed to notice something glistening on the side of the chopper. He bent down and removed a small black metal object and examined it.

"A tracker, really? You thought we wouldn't notice. This ridiculous little show and now some needless extra bruising for nothing." Winter didn't attempt to hide his arrogance. "I would have thought you would have seen the pointlessness of trying to follow me. I survive and succeed because I'm a professional. Like my colleagues, I'm well versed in my craft. I will leave no trail for you to follow. You two would do well to remember that."

Winter looked at us like we were a couple of failed cadets.

"However did you two last so long in such dangerous occupations?" he said dismissively as he climbed on board. "You will be hearing from me."

Greatrex and I must have looked crestfallen as we stared up and watched the departing helicopter. At least we hoped we would.

"How many?" I asked.

"Two," he responded. One for him to find, and one where the skids meet the body, much harder to find."

Two trackers, one undiscovered. One small chance to save four lives and perhaps countless more. In my gut I knew one thing was certain. At the end of his operation Giles Winter had no intention of letting any of us live. He'd virtually said it himself: "I will leave no trail for you to follow."

"Winter loves his plans, doesn't he?" observed Greatrex with a wry smile that only those who knew him well would understand.

"He does. He's a real Hannibal Smith," I responded with a half-hearted chuckle.

But I was thinking about something else, someone else. I was thinking about John Lennon. "Life's what happens when you're making other plans," he had sung.

I hoped he was right. All our lives were depending on it.

# Chapter 7

It was nearly midnight when I turned off Ocean Park Boulevard into the quiet side street where Greatrex lived. I felt the warm breath of the dry Californian air on my face as I stepped out of the Jag. There was almost no traffic and the street was eerily quiet.

Greatrex had dropped me off at my apartment to pick up my car after we returned from the Rancho de la Luna an hour earlier.

I'd completed my recording commitments at the studio as quickly as I could. It seemed a waste to rush such an enjoyably creative experience and head straight back to LA, but we had no choice. Our instructions were to carry on normally. Our intentions were to get back here as quickly as we could to see what we could do about chasing down Giles Winter and finding a connection to where Leyla and Amira were held.

Greatrex lived in an apartment on the ground floor of an old gray two-story weatherboard beach house a few streets back from the beach between Venice and Santa Monica. He had the whole ground floor. It was space he needed, for his peace of mind and his work.

I let myself in with my own key and walked to a door at the far end of the hall. This led to Jack Greatrex's private sanctuary. While part of the darkened space featured a digital recording set-up we had both frequently used, the other side of the dimly lit room revealed two enormous wooden sliding doors.

The doors were now wide open and Greatrex sat on a desk chair, focused on the equipment in front to him. The subject of his attention was a variety of audio and visual equipment most people would assume was some sort of digital editing suite. It was not; or rather, it could be, but that was not its main purpose. The equipment Greatrex now manipulated, with great skill and dexterity, was a highly sophisticated military-grade surveillance system.

Greatrex was a tech-head; he always had been, he always would be. His skills had served him well in the military and very well as an in-demand tech in the music industry. I hoped they would serve him equally well now, as we desperately tried to locate an extremely dangerous man who held our two innocent friends hostage.

I pulled up a chair and sat down next to my friend. His eyes were focused on a monitor that showed a Google Earth–style of display with a lone digital marker in the center of the screen.

"That's them." He pointed at the marker on the screen. "Or at least it's the tracker, hopefully still connected to the helicopter."

Of course, a big question was who "them" was. Was it Giles Winter, his henchman, and Leyla and Amira? Was it just Winter and his men? Was it just the helicopter? We couldn't possibly know.

"Where are they?" If there was an obvious question to ask, I was always the one to ask it.

"Oregon, specifically a remote part of the Rogue Valley area."

"How appropriately named," I responded.

Greatrex continued. "The tracker has been stationary since I got back here."

It made a lot of sense to me. The chopper clearly had long-range capabilities. Slipping back over the state line to Oregon would have been simple. It also connected with the fact that Winter had kidnapped Leyla and Amira from their home in Portland, Oregon. He obviously felt no need to move them too far away at this point.

Greatrex turned to me. "What now?"

Strategy had usually been my end of the partnership. At this point, however, I was tired and frustrated; brilliant ideas were not appearing at the speed of light. There was a long silence between us as we were both lost in thought.

An array of alternatives began to flash across my mind as my brain began to focus. The trouble was that the former military strategist in me dismissed each idea as useless almost as it formed. Maybe it was time for the other side of my brain to kick in, the creative side. There were some advantages to living in my conflicted head. It was time to start sorting through the obstacles.

"We have no choice, we must try something." I said.

Greatrex nodded in agreement. "We were told to carry on as per normal," said the big fella. "We know they're watching us; any move we make out of our routine will endanger the girls."

"You're right on both counts," I answered. "However, there may be a way around that." I thought a little longer before speaking again. "How often have we been booked into the studio to record, and the session has run all day and all through the night?"

As I spoke, I saw a slight look of optimism on Greatrex's worried face.

"What if we arrange with Mac Silverman down at Platinum Sound to book us in for an all-nighter? He would need to set it up on his books and get some other players in to make a noise. We make a show of arriving though the front door and less of a show leaving out the back."

"It would need to look authentic to an outsider," Greatrex said.

"I could offer the session to Robbie as free recording time. Having his 'celebrity' name on it would make the recording look legitimate, and he's always complaining his record company doesn't provide him with enough studio time."

"It might work, but it could be risky."

"It will be risky," I responded, "but I don't see that we have a choice. Up to this point we've been reacting to everything with little or no pushback. We've never worked that way before; I don't reckon it's time to start now." I paused for a few seconds to consider the impact of what I was suggesting. "Winter and his men will be tracking us visually and electronically. I'd bet they're using our cell phones to monitor us when we're out of sight. We will need to leave the phones at the studio. The downside is we'll be out of contact if Leyla should have an opportunity to contact us. The upside is we'll be able to work in the shadows." I was really starting to think now, about goddamn time.

Greatrex chipped in. "That will still only give us a twenty-four-hour window at best from arriving at the studio to get up to the Rogue Valley and try and get the girls out, if they are there."

"We also need to allow time to get back if Leyla and Amira

aren't there. If Winter discovers we've slipped under the radar for any length of time, I don't think he'd hesitate to harm them."

"I have an old military friend," said Greatrex. "He was a chopper pilot in Afghanistan and Iraq. These days he runs a helicopter charter service out of Burbank. If he's available, he'll get us there and back quickly, and off the books."

Jack Greatrex was one of the best-connected people on the planet. He never ceased to amaze me. People just seemed to like him and want to help him out.

"You contact your friend, I'll get hold of Robbie, and Mac at the studio. We have to make this happen fast to have any chance of success. Oh, and of course, we can't use our phones."

Again, before my eyes the best-resourced man in the world conjured some extra magic. Greatrex reached into his pocket and brought out two prepaid cell phones, still in their packaging.

"I bought these at the supermarket after I dropped you off. I thought we may find a need for them."

I stared at the two burners, grateful for my friend's forethought.

No more planning required, we went straight into action. It sounds good when you say it like that: "straight into action." Both Greatrex and I were aware, however, that every action invites a reaction. That was our worry.

# Chapter 8

Things had gone smoothly down at Platinum Sound. Everybody had arrived at the Culver City studio on time. The musicians were a bit perplexed at the short notice for the session, although this wasn't that unusual in our industry. Robbie West couldn't really understand why I couldn't stay and play. There was no way we could explain the circumstances to any of them, particularly Robbie, who was extremely likable but also very talkative.

Greatrex and I made our exit out the side door of the loading bay at the rear of the building. So much gear was going in and out, no one noticed us leaving. We had used the studio credit card to book a hire car and have it delivered two streets away. We found it easily, climbed in, and headed north toward Burbank.

The traffic on the 405 was light by LA standards, and we began to make good time. So far, so good, although one thing was for certain: we'd have a lot of explaining to do to our musical colleagues when this was over. Fifty minutes later, we were parking our hire car in the car park of the Hollywood Burbank Airport.

We quickly located the hangar that was the base of Greatrex's friend Eddie Small. Eddie was waiting at the front of the building. A short man with dark curly hair and a jovial smile, Eddie quickly ushered us around the back and into his sleek silver chopper.

"The less people that see you, the less questions will be asked," said Eddie as he shook my hand.

"I've logged this flight as two investors looking for real estate in Northern California and Southern Oregon." Eddie then chuckled as he said, "If anyone asks, your names are Bill Oates and Simon Hall."

Greatrex smiled. "You just couldn't help yourself, could you, Eddie?" he said, referring to the musical connection. It was a welcome break from our stress. Passengers Hall and Oates lifted off five minutes later.

As the sun was beginning to set, three and a half hours later, Jack Greatrex and I were hiking through tall ponderosa pines as we headed toward the Rogue River. Eddie Small had dropped us off in a vacant paddock near the Riverbanks Road just south of Shan Creek.

It was an area full of small acreages and hobby farms. Enough people around for newcomers not to stand out, remote enough to lose yourself in, affluent enough so choppers flying in and out wouldn't cause a fuss. Giles Winter had chosen a perfect location for his criminal retreat.

We had used the coordinates provided by the tracker on Winter's helicopter to establish our destination, and a portable GPS in Greatrex's hand allowed us to find our way there. We avoided established roadways as and when we could.

Fifteen minutes later and we were perched on a small hill looking down through thick scrub at a well-kept stone and wood lodge-style building. The place was rustic and seemed quite luxurious. A long, treed circular drive led from the road to the front door. The Rogue River ran one hundred yards distant from the main building. There were two machinery sheds behind the house, one large enough to house a helicopter. We knew this because the doors were open and inside the shed was a large black helicopter with no markings.

"Bingo," said Greatrex.

The house lights were on in a couple of rooms, but we couldn't see any movement.

"We need to think this through carefully. If they're all there, it will be Winter, the girls, and at least three very heavily armed men." I needed to show that I could do the math.

"There may be more," said my friend, always the optimist.

We were both as keen as all hell just to storm down the hill and take our chances, but that would put Leyla and Amira at great risk if we didn't make it. It would put us at great risk either way.

"We could wait and call the local police," suggested Greatrex. I knew that wasn't what he wanted to do, but we had to consider all possibilities.

"By the time they got here, we explained ourselves, and any action was taken if the cops did believe us, Winter and the girls would be forewarned and long gone."

Greatrex seemed relieved at my response.

"You skirt around the north side to the back and see what you can find," I suggested. "I'll recon the front and river side. We'll meet back here in twenty minutes. No excitement until we have a plan."

Greatrex had disappeared into the scrub before I could say another word. He was like that.

Fifteen minutes later I was back on top of the hill. I had seen nothing to indicate any human movement, but I had also seen nothing that indicated the property was vacant. There were lights on and what sounded like a television coming from inside. This made the scenario very uncertain. I didn't like uncertain; uncertain was dangerous.

I then spent a good five minutes just watching from the hill, looking for any sign of movement.

In the silence and the waiting, my mind started working me over. Things were changing, beyond my control. I hadn't been given a choice. I left the armed forces because I wanted to have choices. I wanted to be my own moral compass, not the instrument of someone else's perspective. It suited me, being a musician, and it had turned out I was pretty good at it. It was not a life I sought to give up. It worried me that my old military skills had rebooted so quickly, like they were always there but just out of sight. It worried me that my sense of right and wrong had steered me back here. What worried me the most was the last thing I had said to Jack Greatrex before he set out on his recon: "no excitement." The thing that was really eating away at me as I looked down on a potentially life-ending and dangerous situation was ... I was excited.

My self-examination finished abruptly when Greatrex appeared from the bushes behind me.

"I couldn't see anyone, but I couldn't not see anyone," he said.

"You know there's only one way we are going to find out, and the clock is ticking." I didn't even begin to like the words as they came out of my mouth.

"We go in."

"We go in," I repeated. "You take the back, I'll go front. Coordinated entry. When you hear me go in the front door, you go through the back. There's no point in stealth once we enter. We search each room quickly, take out whoever is standing." Nicholas Sharp taking command.

"And be careful of the girls," I added. I looked down on the house one last time. It had been a long time since I'd been involved in events like this. Even then, I was more comfortable working at a sniper's distance, not up close and intimate.

I gave Greatrex five minutes to take up position. I then followed a line of pines down the south side of the hill, keeping in the shadows as much as possible. The distance from the last tree to the front door was a good fifty feet; I would be very exposed but there was nothing I could do about it. Once I was out of the shadows I moved as speedily as I could without making a lot of noise. The gravel driveway didn't help. I seemed to reach the wooden railed veranda undetected. At least I hoped so.

Thanks to Greatrex I had two handguns on me. I withdrew one from my pocket and held it in front of me. I had a long-range rifle up on the hill, but it would be useless to me here. Greatrex was similarly armed but also had a sawn-off shotgun. I didn't know where he got it; I hadn't asked. We weren't in the military anymore, yet Greatrex still managed to procure things.

I waited for a minute to listen for any sound that would indicate something. There was no sound. I took a deep breath and …

In the stillness of the early evening the crack of the front door being kicked open sounded like a small explosion. Two seconds later the back door was kicked open; it was incredibly loud as well. Greatrex was also in. In the heat of the moment it took several seconds before I realized why both doors had sounded like explosions through the night. They *were* explosions—the doors were rigged to trigger detonations around the house, and the building was starting to burn.

I moved through the entrance hall into the lounge, my gun arm leading the way. No one was there. I was relieved we weren't walking straight into a firefight, but worried that I could see no sign of Leyla and Amira. I moved through the dining room into the large wooden and slate lodge-style kitchen. If I was an LA cop I would have been yelling "clear" in every room. I wasn't, so I didn't.

As I left the kitchen another explosion echoed through the house. It came from the lounge room. Then there were two more in quick succession. The whole house was rigged.

"Jack, are you all right?" I yelled above the cacophony of sound.

"I'll go upstairs, you stay down," he yelled back. "I reckon we have less than two minutes before the whole place goes up."

I went from room to room, no longer caring about men with guns. I was only focusing on finding the girls before the house was destroyed. More explosions, more rooms, fire everywhere. Time was running out and the heat and the noise were unbearable.

As I entered the final downstairs room, I could see that it was a bedroom. I could also see two sets of chains with shackles attached to the double bed in the center of the room. The bed was now on fire, and there was no one in the shackles. Leyla and Amira were here, but they had gone. We were too late.

"Jack, get out," I screamed up the stairs. "They aren't here."

Greatrex came—almost falling, almost flying—down the stairs. For a big man he moved very quickly. We both burst out the back door at the same time. We were gasping for air, coughing, choking on smoke. Behind us, the house was

47

fully ablaze. If anyone was in there now, they would have no chance.

Greatrex looked at me, his blackened face confused.

"Why?" he asked. He was having trouble getting words out between coughs and gasps. "Why would they destroy this place?"

"No trail," I gasped, echoing Winter's words. I was having the same trouble speaking and breathing.

It took a good five minutes until we seemed in control of ourselves. Then a thought occurred to me. "The chopper. We might find something useful in the chopper."

We both turned and took a step toward where the black helicopter loomed among the darkness in its shed. The next thing I knew, I was flying backward through the air and flung mercilessly to the ground. This explosion was so loud it made the others sound like backyard fireworks. When I sat up and looked over to the shed, both Giles Winter's helicopter and the shed had disappeared in an eruption of flame and smoke. Beside me, Greatrex was regaining his senses.

We must have sat there on the ground forever, I didn't know what Greatrex was thinking but I had a fair idea. I knew what I was thinking. If we had moved toward the helicopter shed thirty seconds earlier, I would be testing my theory of what it was like to meet God after shaking Paul McCartney's hand.

It also hit me like a stack of bricks that we had lost Leyla and Amira. We had lost the one chance we had of locating them. We may also have alerted Winter to our poorly attempted work in the shadows. I prayed that this was not the case. If it was … oh God, what had we done?

# Chapter 9

Everybody has a bar—well, it seems that way—a place where you go to drink, talk, feel comfortable, take refuge, celebrate, commiserate. Everybody has a bar, and mine was Medina's. On Washington Boulevard, not far back from Venice Beach and walking distance from my apartment, Medina's was a two-story painted stucco building typical of restaurants and bars in the area. Typical except for one thing: it had history; we had history.

Kenny Medina was one of my best and most trusted friends, a generation older than me. Kenny was also my mentor, at times my guide and always one hell of an inspiration. It seemed like there was nothing Kenny hadn't done. When he was younger, he played in bands, some of them quite successful. He then moved on to become the king of piano and lounge bars around LA. Kenny was always in demand; he could make any audience feel like family. People from all backgrounds—rich, poor, black, white, and everything in between—had sat around Kenny's piano pouring their hearts out. In time, like all good entrepreneurs, Kenny had done his own thing and opened his own bar. Much of the West Coast music industry immediately adopted Medina's as their own.

When I arrived in LA after leaving the military, I was shaken and confused. I would spend my days pounding and caressing the piano in my apartment until I felt my balance slowly return. Then one evening I found Medina's. Then I kept finding it. One night, as I was going through a particularly dark period, I asked if I could have a play of the bar's beautiful Kawai grand piano. Thirty minutes later I looked up, the room was silent, everyone was staring at me.

Kenny Medina walked up, introduced himself and said, "Son, I've got Monday nights free; they're yours if you want them."

There you have it: Nicholas Sharp, former Marine sniper, now paid professional musician.

One thing had led to another, and contact after contact was made through Kenny and his bar. Five years later I was recording and touring the world at a level of success I never dreamed of. Who would have thought?

I owed Kenny Medina big-time.

Medina's was my bar.

I sat in one of the booths in Medina's downstairs room, checking out the framed pictures that lined the walls, every one of them taken in-house. The famous, the legends, the young bloods, from Keith Richards to Ray Charles, Muddy Waters to Norah Jones—a lot of wonderful musicians had made Medina's their bar for at least one night. My mind, however, wasn't on them; I was nursing a scotch and waiting for Jack Greatrex. Jack wasn't late, I was just anxious.

"You look like hell." It was Greatrex's voice.

"I look like hell because that's where I'm living right now."

Greatrex sat down opposite me as a Heineken was delivered to our table. He looked no better than me.

It was twenty-four hours since we'd returned from our escapade to Oregon. As we left we had managed to elude all the official authorities arriving in response to the fire and explosions at the property beside the Rogue River. Cutting back through the forest the way we had come, we called Eddie Small, so he was waiting with the chopper at the same place he dropped us off. In all the chaos, one more helicopter landing and taking off in the night went unnoticed.

After arriving at Burbank and saying our thanks and good-byes to Eddie, we hightailed it back to the studio in the rental car. We were back at Platinum Sound twenty-two and a half hours after we left. We had done our best to clean ourselves up, but to some extent our picture must have told the story. Our musician colleagues had the good grace not to ask us any questions, but somewhere down the line they were going to.

Greatrex and I sat here looking at each other across the table, the same huge question hanging over us both. Did Giles Winter know we had discovered and invaded his property?

"It's been twenty-four hours. You would think if Winter knew we were there, we would have heard from him by now," I said.

"You would think," Greatrex responded, "but we have to work this through. Were the explosions all on a timer and they just happened to go off as we entered the building? Did we trigger the explosions as we entered? Or, of course, the worst-case scenario, did Winter have someone watching the property and they set the explosions off when they saw us go in?"

"They had to be rigged to explode on entry," I said. "If it had been anything else, we would have known by now."

It had been an agonizing twenty-four hours, waiting for the phone call telling us either Leyla or Amira were dead because of our actions.

"We're not out of the woods on this one," I continued, "but let's work on the theory we got away with it." I needed to believe this for my own mental health.

"If they were going to blow up the buildings and the helicopter anyway, the question would be why," said Greatrex.

"I've been thinking about this one," I began. "We know from what Winter told us about his network that they are well resourced. The cost of losing that property and the chopper, if they owned them, would have been of no consequence. What would have been of consequence to Winter was that we had seen the chopper and may, just possibly, figure out a way to identify or track it."

"Then he planned all along to dispose of them."

"I think so. He virtually told us that's how he operates. His mark is that he leaves no mark. Nothing for us to follow." I looked around the room. "I think the bottom line here is that Winter felt he needed to take the girls and do the ultimate 'vanish without a trace' bit. That's why he destroyed that place. That also confirms that we were probably right in thinking that he has no plans to let Leyla, Amira, you, me, or anyone else connected with this mess live past their usefulness to his plans. When this is all over, he will 'vanish without a trace,' and so will we."

"We can't let that happen."

I appreciated Jack Greatrex's determination.

"No, we can't let that happen," I echoed. "The trouble is, right now, I can't think of one way to stop him."

Greatrex signaled to Joey, the barman, for two more drinks.

Two hours and several drinks later we were still sitting at our booth in silence. The house band was playing a Marvin Gaye classic, but as good as they were sounding, we weren't really listening. We were each lost in our dark world of nightmare possibilities. We had lost complete control of the situation. We had no plan except to sit and wait for Giles Winter to contact us and, like some dark puppeteer, let him control our next moves.

The last strains of "I Heard it Through the Grapevine" were playing when the faintest idea started to develop in my mind. Greatrex must have seen a changed look on my face.

"What?" You can't hide much from the big fella.

"It's probably nothing, but ... we've been concentrating on finding Leyla and Amira and making them safe, right?"

"Right." I could see that he thought I might be losing the plot. I thought I might be losing the plot.

"Let's go back to thinking about the long game."

Greatrex took a sip of his drink and nodded.

I continued, "If Winter plans on getting those chemical weapon and nerve agent samples into our gear, then he will need someone on the inside of the touring crew to do it."

A flicker of light in Greatrex's eyes.

"We know the army personnel will be keeping close watch over the equipment—guarding it, in fact—to ensure no bombs, explosive devices, et cetera, are planted there," I said.

"True."

"Now, you and I know how this works," I said. "Any army personnel caught tampering with the gear would look immediately suspect. They are there to guard it, not play with it. We know we will have our civilian road crew working with us. It makes some sense that one of them might be Winter's man."

"Even accounting for using army riggers for the stage and towers, there will be at least forty civilians working that tour, and you and I don't know all of them personally." Greatrex made a good point.

"You're right," I thought for a moment, "but chances are whoever is Winter's inside person will have joined the crew at the last minute, a ring-in with the right skills."

"How could we know who that was? We don't do the crew rostering; your management won't even know." Greatrex had another point.

I took a long, comforting sip of my drink. I felt some positive energy return. "I think Marvin Gaye is going to help us here."

At this point I think Greatrex must have concluded that I had totally lost any sense of reality.

"Maybe you should ease up on that scotch, Nick."

I smiled. "That last song the band played, 'I Heard it Through the Grapevine,' that's it."

Greatrex had clearly given up on me.

"The crew we are using comes from LA. Who hears everything that is going on in the music industry in this town?"

First Greatrex smile in five minutes. "Kenny Medina?"

"Kenny Medina," I repeated. "Kenny may not know that the tour is going to Iraq, but he knows we are touring. If there are any major changes in our touring crew, last minute or otherwise, I bet my best keyboard Kenny would hear about it."

"Kenny Medina," repeated Greatrex.

We looked up and saw the slightly worn but warm, smiling face of Kenny Medina, framed by his longish dark hair turning a distinguished gray. He was walking toward our table.

"Nick, Jack, how's it going, guys?"

I looked up and grinned.

Medina's is my bar.

# Chapter 10

The next five days went past without incident. Still a lot of worry, little sleep, and ridiculous stress levels, but no incident. We were starting to feel more confident that our sojourn to the Rogue Valley had not caused any major repercussions. Since Oregon we had followed our original instructions and just carried on with our normal existence, at least outwardly.

I had two sessions at two different studios during those five days. Jack Greatrex and I followed our usual pattern of him getting to the studio an hour before me to set up my keyboards, and guitars if necessary. I would arrive twenty minutes before each session, grab a coffee and meet with the session producer to be briefed. Sometimes, if we were just doing keyboard overdubs, I would be the only musician there. On other occasions, if we were putting down band tracks, there would be several musicians present. For these two sessions I was the only one recording. This involved a great deal of focus over several hours of intense work creating keyboard parts, precisely fitting in with the band tracks already recorded and responding to the producer's ideas and vision. To be honest, I was glad of the distraction.

My manager, Wayne De Soto, had called to see if I was available to work on an album for an up-and-coming female singer-songwriter the following month. I had heard of her, and she was good. She wanted to do some co-writing as well as getting me to record keyboard parts. It was the sort of work I really enjoyed, as it gave me a chance be a little more original and creative. According to the calendar, I would be back from the tour by then, so Wayne thought timing would not be a problem. I agreed and let him book it for me. Looking at forward dates seemed to bring everything to a disquieted head in my mind; I desperately hoped I would be around to fulfill those dates. I also knew that the chances of that were growing slim if Greatrex and I didn't start being proactive and think of a way to challenge Giles Winter's plans for us.

We had heard nothing from Kenny Medina until the afternoon of the fifth day, when he called.

"I have some information on your touring crew that may be helpful."

"I'll be in tonight," I responded. I was booked at Medina's this evening to fill in for the keyboard player in the house band, who had another gig. The money wasn't much but I loved playing at the bar.

"See you tonight," my old friend said, and hung up.

By then it was late afternoon and Greatrex and I were back at my apartment overlooking the golden sands of Venice Beach and staring out to the vast blue waters of the Pacific Ocean. We were still restless and frustrated. Yet again we were discussing different, seemingly pointless options. I told him about Kenny's call.

"It may not be much, but it's better than anything we have," he observed.

"Anything is better than nothing."

The sound of my phone interrupted us and signaled that a

text message was waiting for me. I reached for it but did not like what I saw.

"Mr. Sharp, you will require a space of the following dimensions within your equipment to store our package. Manufacturer's specifications show that with a little adjustment there will be room within the casing of your Nord stage piano. Please get Mr. Greatrex to arrange this." The specifications followed. The message concluded with, "There is no point trying to trace this message," and was signed GW. I showed the phone to Greatrex.

"The devil continues to conduct." he said.

"And we continue to play. Is he right? Can you create that space within the keyboard?"

"It will be tight, but there is room. Winter has done his research. I'll organize it."

The reality was starting to sink in that we may well end up importing deadly chemical weapons and nerve agents into the US. Every musician likes to be remembered, but being a courier for terrorists and threatening the security of my homeland with mass murder was not the immortality I had in mind.

We were both feeling the same thing. Three days to go until the tour started, only the possibility of Kenny Medina's slim information to work with. We really were being played.

That evening Medina's was jumping. It was warm and hectic in the bar, and a large crowd was enjoying the soulful stylings of the house band. These were a bunch of musicians I loved playing with, not only very capable technically, but also with an intrinsic understanding of the groove and space that were required to play soul and funk. This was something that could not be taught. Kenny had caught me at the beginning of the evening to say he would fill me in on what he had found out when the crowd thinned, and he could take a break from being the busy maître d'.

After a very satisfying version of James Brown's "Gravity," the band headed for a break in a booth set aside for that purpose. I joined my colleagues, scotch in hand. I was chatting with Suzie, the band's outrageously good singer, about the state of the local music industry, when Kenny Medina caught my attention and waved me over. As I left the band table my mind switched immediately to far more serious matters than who was getting what gigs in town. I went through a door behind the bar and into Kenny's private office.

"How are you coping, Nicholas?"

"Frustrated, but glad of the diversion of playing tonight." We had filled Kenny in on the basics of our situation, but we had not mentioned Giles Winter. We didn't want to put Kenny in harm's way. He knew enough, however, to know we had a serious problem.

"I have a little information. I don't know how helpful it will be to you, but it was all I could find out."

"Please," I said, "any information is a beginning." I think Kenny sensed the desperation in my voice.

"Well, most of the crew working on your tour are people you normally work with when you tour with Robbie West. Also, they are keeping the numbers fairly tight, and no one is talking much. I don't want to know the details, but to me this says there may be a USO component to some of your shows."

Kenny was very perceptive. USO stood for United Service Organizations. They were the people who provided live entertainment to members of the United States Armed Forces and their families. They were also the people who were organizing the Iraq leg of our touring schedule.

I nodded and said nothing.

"As I thought," Kenny continued. "There have, however, been two new additions to the crew at this late stage. One is Tommy Dabbs as foldback operator."

I knew of Tommy Dabbs. He had a reputation for always delivering a fantastic foldback sound on stage. Foldback was how musicians could hear themselves when they performed; a good stage sound was very important to a musician. I seemed to recall that Tommy had also had a little trouble with authorities at some point. It surprised me that he would be employed on a USO tour. I mentioned this to Kenny.

"I thought this also, Nick. Apparently, the issue to which you refer was sorted out quietly a while ago, and there is no official record of it, hence his employment."

Although proof of nothing, the Tommy Dabbs situation did cause me some concern. I was certainly going to keep a close eye on him while we were away.

"The other late addition," continued Kenny, "is Kaitlin Reed as tour manager."

I knew Kaitlin; I'd worked with her before. She was very good, very efficient, and very attractive. I couldn't see any immediate problem with her being on the tour.

"Thanks, Kenny. As usual you seem to have a handle on everything that goes on in the music industry in this town. This may all be nothing, but it may be a big help."

Kenny gave me the same warmhearted smile that had won him the hearts and trust of so many. "Nick, I don't know the depth of your problems here, but I can tell from your face you are very concerned. I know from your past that you can handle yourself, but ... please be very careful." He then laughed.

"Besides, good piano players are hard to find."

I left Kenny Medina sitting at his desk, looking like a concerned uncle, as I went back to join the band for the final set.

I was keen to get back to Greatrex's place to let him know what I had found out. I wanted to hear his thoughts. Jack, however, was home in his workshop making the requested adjustments to my favorite touring keyboard. In the meantime, I would have to bury myself in the diversion of playing some good music with some great musicians. It was certainly better than being drawn into the dark vortex of uncertainty that seemed to be my future.

# Chapter 11

The next day, couriers organized by the USO arrived at my door to pick up the keyboards, guitars, amplifiers, and extraneous equipment we were using on the tour. In a couple of days Greatrex and I were being flown to Washington, the official departure point for the tour. It was, however, more economical for the heavier equipment to travel by road. The two of us helped the couriers load the equipment into their van. Everything was in heavy-duty road cases, but we still gave them the standard musician's lecture about looking after sensitive gear. We weren't convinced of their sincerity when they said they would take great care with it, but we had no choice. Inside one of the cases was my red Nord stage piano with the cavity Greatrex had created. It was empty now, but it was with a heavy heart that I thought about what it may contain when we returned home.

Two days later, after a raft of last-minute preparations, Jack Greatrex and I sat in the back of a cab leaving Venice and heading to LAX for our flight to Washington. We didn't say much; we knew we were heading into the frantic and talkative environment of a busy tour. Sitting silently in the back of the cab, gazing at the chaotic LA traffic, gave us a chance to attempt to come to terms with the events ahead of us. We had already over-discussed every possible combination of events and every possible scenario we could think of. Now it was time to let it all play out and hope we could influence the outcome.

We met the rest of the band and some of the touring party at LAX. Many of the crew had gone on ahead to look after the equipment that had gone by road. As I walked into the VIP lounge at the terminal I was greeted by Brian Pitt, our drummer. Brian is one of those people who always seem to make the most of every situation and see the best in everyone. We were good friends and I was glad to see him.

"Hey man, how cool is this, Nick?" he chortled happily. "Traveling around the world, guarded by the military, going into a war zone—if only my ex-wife could see me now!" Sometimes it seemed every musician had an ex-wife. Brian had three.

"It sure will be an experience," I responded. I never lied to my friends.

"Hello, Nick." It was Robbie West, looking every bit the rock star on tour. He was surrounded by some attentive young ladies, signing a couple of autographs and looking extremely happy that his era and style of music had come back into fashion.

"Hey, Robbie." I couldn't help but like him; he was one of the few "stars" who seemed to really appreciate those who worked with him.

"Nicholas Sharp."

I turned around to see a tall blonde woman dressed in tight jeans and a loose cheesecloth top. She had piercing blue eyes, extremely long legs and a stunningly beautiful face.

"Kaitlin," I responded. "I heard that you'd joined the tour."

A moment of hesitation crossed her face, but then it was gone. She leaned forward for a kiss on the cheek.

I obliged.

"Great to see you, Nicholas."

"You too," I responded, and meant it.

From across the room Jack Greatrex gave me an all-knowing look and half a smile.

Before we could reminisce, a muffled voice through the lounge speakers called our flight for boarding. We all picked up our things and headed toward the departure lounge. One of the great things about working in a celebrity world is first-class travel; it's all about minimal waiting and being well looked after.

Forty minutes later, as the huge jet engines of Virgin America flight 1108 blasted us into the air, our plane turned east and headed toward Washington DC. We had five hours of flying time ahead of us just to get to the place where we were going to depart from. I knew there would be some drinks, some seat swapping and a lot of catching up. I was happy with that; I was done with my own thoughts.

I couldn't help but notice Kaitlin Reed two seats behind me, looking in my direction. Was this good, or was it an issue? I had no reason to suspect it was anything but good. On the other hand, my trust in humanity and all things positive had been severely scarred in the last couple of weeks. I was suspect of everything and trusted nothing. I then heard Greatrex laughing in the row ahead of me. He was sitting next to our bass player, Barry Flannigan, enjoying one of the veteran musician's many tales of life on the road.

Nicholas Sharp, conflicted man … again. I made the decision to put all my cheerless thoughts to one side and ordered a scotch.

Fly me to the moon.

# Chapter 12

It seemed like no time at all, and our wheels were touching down at Washington Dulles International. We had done all the catching up we needed on the plane, so there was little conversation as we left the space-age architecture of the airport terminal for the next brief leg of our journey. Several black Humvees were waiting for us on the terminal access road outside. There were no armed forces markings on them, but to someone in the know they reeked military. Greatrex and I were in the know. In the midafternoon sun our convoy wound its way through McLean and Annandale toward Prince George's County in Maryland. Our destination was the Joint Base Andrews.

Although I'd left the Marines several years before, I felt a little uneasy as we pulled up to the Andrews main gate. It was though I was crossing a line. Sitting next to me, Greatrex looked as if he was feeling the same.

A shared look and a shrug, and we were through security and onto one of the most famous military installations in the US. Joint Base Andrews was a relatively recent merger of the Andrews Air Force Base and the Naval Air Facility Washington. The name was new, but the facility's military history was significant.

Brian and the other band members in our Humvee seemed quiet and, if anything, a little in awe. It was not every day a musician's life led them to a place like this. Kaitlin Reed was in the Humvee ahead of us, so I couldn't see her reaction.

Our Air Force driver turned to us and said, "Our instructions are to take you directly to your transport."

No mucking about; we were back in the military now.

On a base that is nearly seven square miles in size and home to many different military units, "direct" is a relative word. As we ventured through the maze of buildings and checkpoints, everyone's eyes seemed to be searching for the most famous aircraft in the world that calls Andrews home. There was, however, no sign of either of the two Boeing 747-200Bs that use the call sign Air Force One while the President of the United States is aboard. Either he was somewhere else or not traveling today. A bit frustrating for the tourists in our party.

We endured a last checkpoint before we were driven out onto the airfield.

On the tarmac ahead of us was the enormous gray shadow of a US Air Force Boeing C-17 Globemaster III military transport aircraft. This is how US armed forces traverse the globe. The C-17 before us was an indication that the civilian part of our journey was behind us.

At the rear of the aircraft the massive ramp was down, and our equipment was being loaded on board. Road cases sitting on pallets covered by heavy-duty webbing were the order of the day. While military personnel were doing the loading with an array of different vehicles, some of our civilian crew who had flown in ahead of us were overseeing the process. As we climbed out of our air-conditioned vehicles into the hot afternoon sun, we could hear some interaction between the two groups.

"Careful of that, dude. That mixing desk is worth more than you earn in a year." It was the voice of our sound operator, Glenn Martinez. The look he received from the two military guys loading the pallet was thinly disguised frustration at best. Two different cultures meeting, working together, but certainly not understanding each other. I began to think that our greatest danger on this tour may not be the insurgents, or even Giles Winter, but the cultural ravine I saw before me.

"Take no notice of him; he's a temperamental buffoon." Our chief lighting engineer, Dennis Scutt, was soothing the waters. Maybe this would work out after all.

Off to one side I noticed a sulky shape I recognized as Tommy Dabbs. He seemed to be securing some gear while watching the others load. My immediate instinct was distrust. Did it look like he was up to something or was distrust just my default setting? I still felt uneasy.

"Right, everyone on board." It was the authoritative voice of Kaitlin Reed, taking charge in an environment full of people in charge. I couldn't help but admire her.

Just as she spoke, a jeep painted in military camouflage coloring pulled up. A man got out: early thirties, sleazy grin, civilian clothes, Ray-Ban sunglasses, good-looking in the conventional sense, and a look of supreme confidence. My feeling was instant dislike. Nicholas Sharp, judgmental bastard.

I whispered to Greatrex, who was next to me, "Who's the used-car salesman?"

Before Greatrex could respond, our new acquaintance walked straight up to Kaitlin and shook her hand, holding it a little too long.

"Elliot Brooks," he introduced himself. "I'm your USO liaison for the tour."

Kaitlin introduced herself and then took him over to Robbie, who was standing in the shade of the aircraft's wing, looking bemused.

"Mr. West … Robbie. I'm Elliot Brooks, your …"

"Yes, USO liaison. Pleased to meet you," said Robbie, although he didn't look that sure that he was.

I was starting to respect our singer's ability to judge character.

"Now, can we get everyone on board please," commanded Brooks.

I'm sure I saw Kaitlin wrinkle her nose as he said it. This could be fun.

As we entered the aircraft through the forward door, the plane seemed to tower above us. Both Greatrex and I knew there were going to be groans of disappointment from our colleagues who were traveling military style for the first time. We were not wrong, there were no comfortable airline seats, no overhead lockers and, more to the point for a bunch of musicians, no stylish flight attendants to pamper us. There was a row of pull-down seats against the wall of each side of the aircraft, and a few additional seats bolted in the middle. The cabin had no windows but a lot of space for our equipment.

Most people seemed a little perturbed. Even Brian seemed to lose his boyish optimism. Robbie West was fine; he'd done all this before, way back when …

As I squeezed past Elliot Brooks, he seemed to be doing his best to impress Kaitlin.

"Now, I'm sure everybody will get used to this," he said. "If you're worried about anything, just ask. I've done a lot of tours, so I'm fairly battle hardened."

I felt the bile sticking in my throat. Brooks then turned to me and held out his hand.

"Elliot Brooks, USO liaison."

"Nicholas Sharp, keyboard player," I returned.

"Don't worry, Nick; this trip won't be as bad as you think. You'll get used to a little hardship in no time."

Bile rising higher. I heard Greatrex chuckle as he sat down. I wouldn't need an M40A5 rifle to take Brooks out from my seat.

My ears must have been playing tricks on me because I was sure I heard Kaitlin whisper to Brooks the words "former Marine sniper."

I may have imagined that I saw Brooks turn a little pale. While being slightly satisfied with the interaction I was also slightly worried. I had never told Kaitlin anything about my military past, and not many people in my new world know about my previous life. How and why did Kaitlin know?

Thirty minutes later we were all on board and the gear was secured. Some other musicians and entertainers who were part of the tour had joined us. They seemed an interesting bunch, but I didn't know any of them. Our US Air Force crew made an appearance, introduced themselves to us, and assured us our eighteen-hour flight to Kuwait, and the following tour, should be uneventful. The engines started, and we began to move.

As we lifted off it really began to hit me. I was going back to Iraq. I was returning to the one place on the globe where I had been forced to confront the bleakest side of humanity, and I was going there under duress. Two of the people I loved most in the world, Leyla and Amira, were being held captive by a madman, their lives in peril if I did not confront this darkness again. I couldn't bear to think about the big picture. What would happen if our reluctant mission for Giles Winter proved successful and we brought his haul of chemical weapons home?

Of one thing I was sadly certain of, this tour was going to be far from uneventful.

# Chapter 13

It was over the mid-Atlantic that the nightmares began.

*I was laying prone on a flat rooftop in Baghdad. The dry heat was overpowering, and I was bathed in sweat. Greatrex was next to me, watching below and watching my back. In my hands was my M40A5 bolt-action sniper rifle. Looking through the scope, I could see our boys were going door to door down a narrow street, clearing each building of insurgent activity. It was my job to protect them. It was my job to be the protector. I was looking for insurgent snipers, bombers, anyone suspicious, I felt uneasy, I could feel something was about to happen. There was a noise on the street that was intersecting with where our Marines were. I know I heard something. Then there was a man; he was holding something, a grenade, a Russian one. I couldn't get a clear shot. He was going to throw it ...*

I woke up. I looked around the large aircraft. Others were either sleeping, using iPads, or talking quietly. I dozed off again ...

*I was playing piano at Medina's. It was a warm evening, and the crowd was into the music. Then there was a crash, the sound of a door being smashed open. I looked up from the piano. There was Giles Winter. In one hand he was holding Leyla with Amira clinging on to her. They were both frightened.*

*"I told you what would happen, Sharp." It was Winter's cold, raspy voice. "This is your doing."*

*Winter's other hand held a rifle—my rifle. He pointed it at Amira.*

*"No, no," I tried to scream, but I couldn't make a sound.*

*Then …*

*Back on a rooftop in Baghdad. It was different this time. It was a different street, different time of day. I was in the same prone position, Greatrex still beside me. Through the scope I saw our men, single file down each side of the street. We had cleared this area before, why were we here again? Again, a noise, a door opened, a man in robes came out. I couldn't see his face, but the Marines did not seem perturbed by his appearance. He offered something to the Marines, or was he about to throw something, or was he just offering his hand? My earpiece crackled, "Do you have a clear shot?"*

*"Yes."*

*"Take it."*

*I found the Iraqi man within my sights. I still couldn't see his face or what was in his hands.*

*"Take the goddamn shot," my earphones crackled again.*

*Orders and reflexes. A soldier's world. I took aim. As I pulled the trigger the Iraqi man turned, as if looking up at me. I wanted to freeze, but I was trained not to. Then I saw the face of Akram Salib disappear into a bloody cloud just as I heard the shot. My shot.*

"Nicholas, Nick, wake up."

I could feel someone shaking me as the hot rooftop and bloody scene in Baghdad receded. I could see Kaitlin's face in front of me.

"That must have been a hell of a dream," she said.

I could see several faces around the plane staring at me.

"Look at you, you're a mess." Kaitlin's concerned face.

I was shivering and covered in sweat. Greatrex was also looking at me from his seat across the plane, his face also wearing concern.

"I guess I just don't like flying," said the conflicted man, just as loud as my voice could make it.

I looked around again; no one seemed to believe me.

For that matter, I didn't believe myself.

The afternoon sun reflected off the hot sands of a desert landscape shrouded in haze as we touched down at Ali Al Salem Air Base, twenty-three miles from the Iraqi border on the Kuwait side. Although owned by the Kuwaiti government, the base was the launching platform for coalition operations in Iraq and Afghanistan. This seemingly endless city of tents and barracks was host to units from across the globe. "The Rock," as Ali Al Salem was nicknamed, was a hub of military activity, day and night.

As we stepped onto the tarmac from the C-17 I felt a wave of oppressive heat envelop me. It was as though we had just stepped into an oven. Although Greatrex and I were expecting it, others in our party who were first-timers in this part of the world were a bit shocked at the extreme temperature.

"It's worse than a packed LA nightclub at 2 a.m. in summer," observed Brian.

"Just keep a close eye on all the guitars," said the ever-observant Greatrex. "Wooden instruments don't take to kindly to the extreme changes in temperature. Moving from cold high altitudes down to the 120 degrees Fahrenheit on the desert floor can warp timber terribly."

At that point every guitarist in our party started worrying about something other than the weather.

Elliot Brooks, the USO man, was talking to some army

personnel a little distance away. Kaitlin Reed had been talking with them as well but walked back to our group.

"We'll be spending the night here before going on to Baghdad in the morning," she said. "The good news is we get VIP accommodation. The bad news is the VIP accommodation is about the same as a campsite, but at least we'll be out of the sun."

Brooks joined us. "Although there is no show booked for here, the commanding officer was wondering if you guys would mind putting on a small acoustic performance for some of the personnel this evening?"

"We are tired, we are hungry, and we are so incredibly overheated," said Robbie West. "Of course we'd love to put on a show; count me in." Robbie the trooper, leading the way.

After a round of "yeah, I'm in" from around the tour party, we were shown to some jeeps that took us to our VIP quarters. Some of the road crew stayed and immediately started working with the military guys to get the gear unloaded and ready for the evening's performance. Maybe the cultural divide wasn't that big after all.

It felt a bit strange being on an US military base but not wearing a uniform. It was almost like Pavlov's dogs. I had not been in uniform or permanently armed for years, yet in this atmosphere I kept feeling underdressed without a flak jacket. Unbelievably, I actually reached down for my rifle a couple of times. Clearly, I was conditioned.

After finding our accommodation, catching a couple of hours sleep, thankfully with no more nightmares, I was awake, showered and ready to prowl. Brian Pitt came with me. Greatrex had gone with the other crew members to set up the equipment, my keyboards in particular. A jeep was waiting to take us to the MWR (morale, welfare and recreation) facility where the performance would be. I was glad because we would probably never have found the place on our own. As we drove past row upon row of tents, I was reminded what our servicemen give up to defend our freedom. Our little visit here was a small inconvenience in the privileged and relatively pampered life I now led. It was as though I was a visitor to my own past.

They say anything that reminds our enlisted personnel of home is a good thing when they're away for months on end. We turned a corner onto what was probably considered the camp's main drag to find a row of sheds that were actually well-known fast food outlets from the States. Even the golden arches were there.

"Who would have thought?" said Brian. He was exploring a brand-new world.

One more corner and we pulled up at the MWR. It was a very ordinary-looking building, simple to construct, simple to deconstruct. Typical military. We entered to find the crew had almost finished the set-up. Greatrex looked exhausted.

"Have some food and head back to our accommodation," I suggested. "It's only an acoustic show this evening. We can get by without you. That's an order."

He gave me the finger. We weren't in the Marines now. "We'll see," he responded.

Kaitlin came over.

"Did you get some sleep?" she asked.

"Enough," I said. "Are we sorted for tonight?"

"We have a starting time and a running order. Everything will be pretty low-key given the impromptu nature of the show," she replied.

"How many people are we playing to?" I was full of questions.

"Around three hundred, enough for a good party."

"Three Marines are enough for a good party," I said smiling. I walked off to find some food before she could respond.

Three hours later we were finishing the last song, one of Robbie's biggest hits. The show was acoustic, but the atmosphere had been electric. Every person in that room had become Robbie West's friend in the course of the evening. He had hosted the show, introduced the other acts, joined in with some of them, got audience members up to sing, and told stories from his home state of California. As John Steinbeck had once commented about entertaining troops abroad, Robbie had gone out of his way to "bring a piece of home to a place full of fear."

We all stayed around for a while talking to military folk and signing anything they wanted autographed. When the word came it was time to head back to our sleeping quarters, none of us were complaining. We were all dog tired yet a little reluctant to leave. I had almost even managed to put out of my mind the dangers of what lay beneath our goodwill visit … but apparently not for long.

We were all being ushered into small buses and jeeps at the side of the makeshift building when Elliot Brooks tapped me on the shoulder. "Nicholas, I believe this jeep is for you," he said, pointing to a vehicle sitting behind the others. I had noticed Brooks talking animatedly to Kaitlin at the end of the show, but I had thought nothing of it until now. I had also noticed Tommy Dabbs not far away from them. I had thought he was trying to listen in without looking like it, but then I thought it was just my imagination.

I climbed into the back seat of the jeep, surprised when no one joined me. As we took off down the small camp "street," surprise turned to mild alarm when the other vehicles turned left, and my driver turned right. Greatrex had slept through the show, as I suggested; suddenly I wished he hadn't and was here with me instead.

"Where are we going?" I asked the driver. "Aren't our quarters in the other direction?" Not that I was certain of that.

"Special orders," said the driver noncommittally.

"Whose special orders?"

No response.

Two minutes later we were pulling up outside another makeshift army hut. It was dark, and all the windows had been blacked out. That wasn't unusual on a military base in the theater of war, but I had a bad feeling. My driver opened the door of the hut, and I went inside.

The interior of the hut was nondescript, mostly bare walls with a few maps scattered around. The roof was canvas, held tight over curved metal rafters, and the floor was wood. A dim light allowed me to see the outline of what I presumed was a man at the other end of the room. Then a brighter light flicked on. I wished it hadn't.

I felt the warm desert night turn ice cold as I saw Giles Winter standing before me.

"Nicholas, you've made it this far. I'm glad you and your friend saw the wisdom in doing what was asked of you."

Once again, I felt anger surge through me, but I wasn't going to let Winter have the satisfaction of seeing me struggle a second time.

"Are Leyla and Amira all right?" I asked, sounding emotionless.

"Fine."

"I want proof." I felt demanding.

"You are predictable, Sharp. Here is a photo," Winter said, offering me his cell phone.

I looked at the picture. Leyla and Amira were huddled together holding a copy of the front page of a newspaper. Their hands were covering the top of the paper, but the date was visible and circled; it was two days ago. I couldn't make out much of the newspaper's masthead, and certainly no words. The girls looked scared but in one piece; thank God for small mercies. I studied the picture for as long as I could, trying to make out any hint or clue it could give me. I closed my eyes, tried to see the picture in my head, and then reopened them. I did this several times. It was an old sniper's trick, the camera-shutter technique. It was about printing the image in my mind. I was also attempting to drag the moment out by looking as forlorn as possible while studying every detail of the photograph. All I could make out was the girls, the date of the paper, and the top of a picture of a couple of men I didn't recognize. Nothing useful.

Winter snatched the phone back. "Now, down to business. Where is Greatrex? I assumed he would be with you."

I explained. Winter seemed to accept my story.

"It was important I see you tonight. For obvious reasons after my last time in Iraq, I am now persona non grata. I am unable to obtain papers or even forgeries to travel freely there."

"My heart bleeds." I understand sarcasm.

"You need to know, however, that I do have a person in country who will be keeping an eye on you and relaying instructions as needed."

Person, not man or woman. No clue given.

"The fact is, things may have gotten slightly more complicated since we last met. We have lost a valuable agent in the field, a small explosives issue, I'm afraid."

"I just don't care, Winter. I don't care who you lose."

"Well you should care, Sharp, because no longer will you simply be passed our samples and the accompanying paperwork. You and Mr. Greatrex will now be required to retrieve them from their original hiding place yourselves."

"You must have lost the plot, Winter; Jack and I don't have the papers to go adventuring around Iraq. We can only stay with the tour." I felt confident with this.

"Not really an issue. A couple of small changes to your itinerary and we can cater for all scenarios."

Small changes to our itinerary. Just how well connected was this man? How far into the military could he reach?

"At the appropriate time you will be instructed as to the location of our goods. You and Mr. Greatrex are resourceful men; you will find a way to retrieve what we need."

"Who is our contact? We need to know who to liaise with." I asked, it was worth a try.

Winter looked amused.

"I will decide what you need to know and when you need to know it. Just do our bidding as requested, and you and your friends will live."

Do our bidding. Who was this guy kidding? He may have been a pretentious pain in the ass, but of one thing I was certain: Giles Winter was a ruthless, dangerous man. He was also a liar.

Before I knew it, Winter was out the door. I followed quickly, but not quickly enough. By the time I had got out the door he had disappeared into the night. The jeep and driver were also gone. Another trail goes dead. We still had no firm idea who Winter's connection was. I kicked the dirt in frustration.

Giles Winter was still pulling all the strings, and now things had become even more complex. Even if we did everything he asked us, there was a good chance we would be caught by the military authorities. The armed forces do not respond well to civilian musicians digging for buried treasure on their patch.

"So sad?" I heard the friendly, mocking tone of Jack Greatrex's voice behind me.

I spun around. "I thought you were back at the room sleeping."

"I couldn't let you loose on your own. I arrived at the MWR just as you were leaving. When I saw you head in the wrong direction, I followed," he explained.

"Well, I just got a serving from Winter. I don't know how he got here or where he disappeared to, but things just got a whole lot more complicated." I filled Greatrex in on the conversation, leaving nothing out.

"More complicated? What chance in hell do we have of pulling all that off?"

"Very little, if any." I was no more optimistic than Jack.

Then that mischievous smile slowly appeared on my friend's face.

"Well, there may be a couple of things I forgot to mention." Greatrex pulled his phone out of his shirt pocket. He passed it over to me. It was a shot of Giles Winter leaving the building where we had just met.

"I took this as he was doing his vanishing into the night bit," he continued. "If nothing else, and the shit hits the fan, we can tie him in to being here tonight. The picture may give us some much-needed credibility." The photo had a date and time stamp on it.

I was pleased. It wasn't a lot, but it was something.

"Oh … one more thing. I managed to have a little chat with your driver before he disappeared."

"And?"

"He wasn't keen to be very talkative at first, but after a bit he seemed to see some reason," said Greatrex.

I knew Greatrex's methods of reasoning when he was crossed.

"And?"

"Our man had instructions to take Winter over to the British unit when he was done with you. That's where he picked him up from an hour ago."

"The British." Wheels were spinning round in my mind, albeit a little too slowly.

"He came in with the British, he's leaving with the British," said Greatrex.

"The British," I repeated. The wheels began to turn faster. I thought back to the photograph, the one of Leyla and Amira with the newspaper. In the back of my mind I knew, I felt, that there was a connection that I just couldn't grasp. I thought I recognized the typeface on the small bit of the masthead I could see under their fingers. I just couldn't place it. Now I could.

"I know where Winter is keeping Leyla and Amira," I virtually shouted to Greatrex. "At least, I know what country they are in, and I would bet money on where they are within fifty square miles."

Greatrex looked confused.

"Where are we playing after the Iraq shows?" I asked.

81

"The Isle of Wight Festival, Southern England."

"Where are the Air Force dropping us off?"

"The RAF Brize Norton base in Gloucestershire, South-West England," he said.

"That newspaper, the one Leyla and Amira were holding. *The Gloucestershire Echo*. I think Leyla had moved her fingers just enough to show me a small section of the masthead print. I think she hoped I might recognize it." I felt my enthusiasm build. "Remember I spent some time in Somerset and Gloucestershire with an English girlfriend when I was on leave way back when? I had told Leyla about it and how much I liked the area and would like to go back."

Greatrex began to nod.

"The girls are being held in the southwest of England. I'm certain Winter will have plans to seize the chemical samples from us there, because we would not expect it. If something goes wrong, he will have Leyla and Amira there to hold over our heads."

My thoughts were becoming more lucid. What I was suggesting just seemed to make sense.

"That also means Winter will want to deal with us at that point as well. Probably during or just after the festival."

"By that time, we'll be out of military hands and his stash will be easier to get to ... and so will we," added Greatrex.

"It's quite a stretch, but for a moment let's assume we're right."

A very small opening, and a tiny amount of luck for the first time in days, thanks to Leyla.

"What can we do with this information, if it is information and not just theory? It's a bit like knowing the time and place of your execution but still being in chains." The big fella had a point.

I thought for a couple of minutes. "Our advantage is the fact that Giles Winter does not know we have figured this out. Somewhere along the line we may be able to use this knowledge as leverage, to try and manipulate a better result. If we are lucky it could be a result in which we all come out of this in one piece."

"In the meantime?" asked Greatrex.

"We do our damnedest to carry out Winter's plan in every possible way," I responded. "We need to if we want to get to England and find the girls."

Greatrex and I looked at each other. We both knew just how hard this was going to be, if it was possible at all. We were also both very aware that the lives we were risking were not just our own, and not just Leyla and Amira's. With the likelihood of chemical weapons falling into the wrong hands, a lot more lives were at stake.

"Despite every chance that this will blow up in our faces, and the dread I'm feeling, there is one more thing," I said.

"What's that?"

"We now have a little hope."

My friend looked up at the dark desert sky and then turned to me; the half-smile returned. "Yes, I suppose we do."

# Chapter 14

The noise of military airport machinery at Ali Al Salem dominated the soundscape as we all stood around on the tarmac watching our US Air Force C-130 Hercules Tactical Transport Aircraft being loaded. It was midmorning of the day following my run-in with Giles Winter. I was still apprehensive of what lay ahead, but hope sprang from the ideas we had formed the night before. At least, they had kept the nightmares at bay.

The C-130 was almost loaded. A smaller plane than the C-17 we arrived in, this prop-powered aircraft had dominated troop transport over shorter distances in the theater of war for decades. I had racked up many hours in them.

Kaitlin called us over to where she was standing with Brooks.

"Elliot has our itinerary for the Iraqi leg of the tour. Please listen carefully." She was almost shouting over the noise.

The schedule of any civilian military tour was never published beforehand. This was for the security not only of the personnel traveling but also of the troops. If a president visited a war zone, America didn't know he was there until he was back. It was just the way it went. We were all ears.

"Well," began Brooks, "there is no need to tell you we are

launching the tour from Kuwait, because we are standing in it."

If he was looking for a laugh, he didn't get one.

"We have had some last-minute changes due to local considerations, but in about twenty minutes we will be departing for Baghdad Airport. From there we will be choppered in to Baghdad itself, the US embassy compound in fact. There will be an evening performance there for armed forces personnel and US contractors. We will, of course, spend the night at the embassy."

Jack Greatrex looked at me. "Changes? Local considerations?"

"Or Giles Winter?" I added.

Brooks continued. "The following day there will be a small performance at the Al-Faw Palace. This will be for government and university dignitaries. Again, we will overnight at the embassy."

I knew the Al-Faw Palace well. It was an incredible building near the Tigris River. Years earlier, when there was a massive coalition presence in Iraq, it had been at the heart of the coalition's Camp Victory headquarters. I understood that it was now being turned into the American University of Iraq, Baghdad. Winning hearts and minds.

"The day after that, our party will again be flown by helicopter from the embassy to the Camp Taji operation base, nineteen miles north of Baghdad. All your equipment will travel by road from the moment we land at Baghdad Airport."

Greatrex and I had both visited the Taji Base briefly in our former roles but didn't know it well.

"We will stage a major performance for personnel at Taji. The audience will include US military personnel, contractors, and Iraqi military from the other side of the base. The brass regard this as a bit of public relations coup."

I whispered to Greatrex, "Nothing like being used for PR fodder."

He barely smiled a response.

Brooks was not done yet.

"While we are to be based at Camp Taji we have also had a request for another acoustic performance, but not at Taji. A small component of our touring group will be flown to an outpost near the town of Al-Qa'im, which is on the Iraqi border with Syria. There are obviously some security considerations involved in this expedition."

Which small component? we all thought.

"Mr. West, I have suggested that as the rest of us are continuing on to Afghanistan, and your group is leaving us at that point to fulfill your commitments in England, that you may want do the Al-Qa'im show."

Subtle.

I looked at Robbie West. He was looking a little unsure because it was obvious this would be the most dangerous section of the trip. He looked around at his band—we all nodded. Robbie was always the good guy, not that he'd been given much choice about it this time.

"Of course we'll do it, Elliot," he responded.

Twenty minutes later we were taxiing down the runway. The C-130 offered the usual airborne military luxury but our minds were no longer on that discomfort. In around an hour we would be landing in Baghdad, Iraq, a place that meant a lot of different things to a lot of different people on that plane. It was a place that filled me with misgivings, trepidation, and conflicted memories. I was sure this visit was going to add another color to that emotional palette.

I was seated between Brian Pitt and Barry Flannigan as the sounds of the four-propeller engines echoed through the aircraft twenty-five thousand feet above the earth. Both looked decidedly nervous; neither had done a military tour to a place of conflict before. It was time for some reassurance.

"Guys, you're both looking a little troubled." Nicholas Sharp, counselor.

"I was reading the US Department of State travel advisory for Iraq last night. Big mistake." Brian did not look happy. "I was okay until it got into the specifics, item number two on the 'if you decide to travel to Iraq' bit."

"What did it say?" Barry sounded a little unsure himself.

"Item number two," repeated Brian, "if you decide to travel to Iraq … make a will."

Barry turned a shade of pale.

"Now, boys, calm down a little here." I was attempting to be the voice of reason. "Time for a little historical perspective. You know the war was over a long time ago. Back in 2011 most US and coalition troops were pulled out; it was virtually all over."

"And then?" asked Brian.

"Islamic State, or Da'esh as the locals know them, built up forces and took over a lot of Iraqi territory."

The teacher had his students' attention.

"That situation was not acceptable to the Iraqi government or the coalition. The Iraqi troops were not yet strong enough to stop them, so they called for help."

"What was the response?" Barry was looking like he was enjoying the story, but only if it was going to be a happy ending.

"Operation Inherent Resolve," I continued. "Our people

went in with many other coalition members. The role was to advise and assist, boost the Iraqi forces' capabilities through training with minimal US troops on the ground involved in direct fighting. There was also some coalition air support."

"I'm thinking I should have paid more attention to the news," said Barry. "What I did see was that we won, didn't we? We beat Islamic State?"

"In Iraq, yes, but only after a lot of damage and the loss of too many lives. Iraq is back in the hands of the Iraqis now, but ..."

"But what?" asked a still nervous-looking Brian. "Why are Americans still advised not to go to Iraq?"

"Islamic State still has influence and strength in some neighboring countries. There remains a lot of insurgent activity throughout Iraq, including Baghdad. The insurgents especially don't like westerners. There's been bombings, murders, kidnapping." Nicholas Sharp, failed counselor.

"But guys, don't worry, you have the entire deployed US military apparatus looking after you. Stay close and do what you're told. We may not have the tens of thousands of troops in Iraq that we had a few years ago, but there are plenty enough there to protect you now." The voice of reason strikes again. The men either side of me looked a little better.

Brian looked at me, "Nick, you seem to know a lot about Iraq. What's up with that?"

I closed my eyes, traveled back a little in time, then looked a little forward—same view. I didn't, or perhaps couldn't, answer my friends.

Our pilot's voice boomed through the intercom. "We have dropped to eighteen thousand feet and will begin our descent shortly. For those of you who haven't done this before, you will have the chance to tell your kids about the infamous corkscrew landing, for those who have … enjoy the ride."

Silence either side of me.

"Just a precautionary measure," I assured my traveling companions. I knew it was a move designed to avoid any surface-to-air missiles or other weaponry attacks on the plane from the ground. I thought it better not to mention this.

As I spoke, the C-130 banked sharply and began descending toward the runway in a slow, tight circle. It was like a spiral staircase or corkscrew to the ground. Before long, without event, we were leveling out and our wheels touched down on the tarmac at Baghdad International Airport.

Because we were a military flight we taxied to the west of the runway, where we pulled up at the New Al Muthana Air Base. This was the military side of the airport, where the Iraqi Air Force was based. It was also used by all coalition members. As the door to the plane opened, I could see Iraqi and US planes sitting on the tarmac. There was a collective sigh of relief around the aircraft.

Kaitlin was first on her feet. Brooks brushed past her, a little too closely I thought, and out the door.

"Everyone up and out," she said. "The military personnel will transfer the gear by road. Our helicopters should be waiting."

And waiting they were; we were getting the VIP treatment. In front of us were two HH-60 Pave Hawk helicopters. These modified versions of the classic Black Hawk were going to ferry us in a couple of trips to the US embassy. Greatrex, Brian, Barry, Robbie, and the rest of our band were ushered into one chopper. We were going in the first load.

The ride was short. Traveling by chopper may have been overkill, but the US military didn't take any chances with VIPs.

The streets of Baghdad were still filled with potential hazards. Some of my colleagues seemed to wince at the sight of the US Air Force crew members manning the chopper's 0.50-inch XM218 machine guns. Precautionary.

A very few minutes later the US embassy compound came into view. It was an enormous mixture of buildings and treed parkland surrounded by the ever-frantic city of Baghdad. The Tigris River wound its way beside it. The embassy was like a city in itself. At 104 acres with over twenty buildings, including six apartment buildings, it was about the size of the Vatican but perhaps a little less holy.

Our helicopter landed smoothly on an area of grass within the compound walls, the second chopper landing next to us. Kaitlin got off the second aircraft and waved us over to a small paved road a short distance away. The helicopters took off instantaneously to pick up more of our touring party. Looking around, it just didn't feel like we were in Iraq, this massive complex seemed like a piece of the United States transported to the Middle East.

A uniformed soldier came over and walked up to Kaitlin, and she introduced herself. "If you follow me, Ms. Reed, I'll show you all to your quarters," he said.

Twenty minutes later we were ensconced in one of the brick apartment complexes. This was certainly more luxurious than the air base in Kuwait, and we each had a room. A map of the whole complex showed a variety of buildings including a gym, a basketball court, indoor pool, and outdoor tennis courts. This certainly was not the Iraq I remembered.

Everyone was looking decidedly more relaxed in this environment; well, everyone except Greatrex and myself. We hadn't had a chance to talk since we left Kuwait and we needed to think through the schedule that had been planned for us.

"How about a walk?" I suggested. We had plenty of time until the equipment arrived, and the show needed to be set up.

"Let's go."

As we walked around the complex, I was still soaking it all in.

"What do you make of all this?" I asked.

"It's quite something, but …"

"But what?"

He went on, "I can't help but feel the Iraqi people had years of Saddam building palaces and monuments to himself. Have we just done the same thing with this embassy?"

"I had similar thoughts. It's funny, though; I hope some good may come out of this."

"What do you mean?"

"Well, tomorrow we play at the Al-Faw Palace. When we knew the place back in the days of Operation Iraqi Freedom, it was a massive military headquarters, and now they are turning it into a university. It seems appropriate."

"In what way?" my friend asked.

Teaching history seemed to be my theme of the day. "Well, Baghdad was once home to the 'House of Wisdom.' It was a major intellectual center during the Islamic Golden Age. From the ninth to thirteenth centuries the House of Wisdom hosted the cream of the intellectual elite. It was the largest repository of books in the world. Up until Saddam took over, the tone in Baghdad was freedom of expression and religious tolerance."

Greatrex looked at me as though I was someone else.

"Sorry, my mother's side," I said. "She believed in a classical education, plus, to be honest, Leyla has provided me with a cook's tour of Iraqi history."

Greatrex looked relieved. "So the US starting a university here has a certain balance and symmetry."

"Exactly," I replied.

We walked some more. The embassy was like an endless maze of buildings and gardens. It was time to change the mood.

"We two philosophers have far more pressing plans we need to attend to," I said.

"Too damn right," agreed the big fella.

"Now we know the itinerary, what do we think? Where are these elusive chemical weapon samples?"

"We know from what Winter said to you that the location is going to be within our tour, geographically speaking." Greatrex had a point.

"We also know from both Winter and Brooks that there was a change to our schedule."

"Apart from adding the side trip to Al-Qa'im, we don't know what the change was." Greatrex making another point.

"I think we can safely assume the samples are not within the walls of this embassy."

"Agreed."

"So," I began, "is it Al-Faw, the Camp Taji operation base, or Al-Qa'im?"

"Hard to know, impossible to be certain."

I continued, "The Al-Faw Palace is a possibility. It was a favorite bolt-hole for Saddam, and he didn't expect to lose it, plus the idea of being near the river creates other access possibilities."

"It was also off limits to the UN inspectors. On the other hand, it's right in the center of Baghdad and was the major coalition headquarters during Operation Iraqi Freedom. Does that seem a likely place to store chemical weapons?"

"Probably not, but we can't rule it out," I said.

"What about Taji? Do you know much about it?"

"Once again, a bit of amateur Iraqi history here, albeit a bit more recent. Al Taji was Saddam's largest and most advanced military base. It was at the heart of his Sunni triangle. Even more to the point, the United Nations Special Commission found six thousand canisters there, built to support chemical weapons. It's common thinking that Al Taji was a major player in Saddam's chemical weapons program."

"Right up to the point the coalition found no chemical weapons."

"Shot a hole in the reason for war," I agreed. "However, the coalition turned Al Taji upside down looking for Saddam's stash, and they found nothing of substance. What are the chances the combined experts of the coalition missed something, and we are going to find it?"

"Almost nonexistent," replied Greatrex.

I nodded. As the afternoon was getting on, there was more activity around the embassy compound. Greatrex would have to go soon and begin setting up the show.

"That leaves Al-Qa'im," I said. "On the positive side the location is near the Syrian border for access, it's easy to get in and out. Presumably, it would be easy to get chemical weapons in and out if things went wrong. Also, I don't know if I read this right, but the Al-Qa'im show seemed like a bit of a last-minute add-on."

Greatrex took over. "On the negative side, things did go pear-shaped for Saddam and Winter, yet neither of them appeared to have been able to arrange someone to cross the border to pick their samples up, if they were there."

"True, that means we're right back where we started."

Greatrex looked at me. "I'll have to go in a minute, but there is one thing we haven't really discussed in any detail yet, the elephant in the room."

"I know," I agreed. "Who is Winter's person on the inside?"

We were both silent, because neither of us had an answer. Just as we were about to start tossing ideas around, the voice of Elliot Brooks intruded.

"Gentleman, there you are. I'm afraid it's time to go."

We looked around. He was walking toward us, accompanied by Kaitlin.

"Can I give you a lift to the basketball arena where we are setting up for the concert, Mr. Greatrex?" Brooks asked.

Greatrex nodded.

"Nicholas, can I have a word with you?" The request came from Kaitlin. She seemed quite earnest.

"Kaitlin, I think you will need to come to the stadium with Jack and myself; they will need you," interrupted Brooks.

Kaitlin looked at me. I'm sure a small wave of fear, or hesitation, or something crossed her face.

"Later," she said looking at me.

"Later," I replied.

I watched the three of them climb into Brooks' jeep and disappear to the other side of the compound.

"Later," I thought. I was puzzled by the brief look I'd seen on Kaitlin's face, and this was not the first time. I was also a little confused about my own feelings toward her. Had we just shared a moment? Yet I wasn't by any means sure I could trust her. When it came to Kaitlin Reed, I wasn't even sure I could trust myself. I did feel we needed to talk; she thought it important too.

Brooks had abruptly put an end to that.
For me, "later" couldn't come soon enough.

# Chapter 15

I looked out at the sea of faces. Around nine hundred people had filled the embassy basketball stadium, and they were going off. We had played well, Robbie had conjured up the "Robbie West magic" and the crowd were totally with us. Before ego took over, I had to remind myself that these folks were working far, far away from home and didn't get that much stateside entertainment. This show, however, was as much of a treat for us as it was for them.

I had tried to catch Kaitlin all evening. Every time I caught her eye someone or something either distracted her or me. I don't know whether I was imagining it, but often as not Brooks seemed to be among the cause of the distraction. For now, I put it down to the frantic atmosphere backstage at a big show.

We were going to finish with a ballad. It was a big song with an anthemic chorus. It had been a huge hit for Robbie, and everyone would know the words. Time to get out the flashlight app on the phones, wave them from side to side, and have a big emotional sing-along. I began the piano introduction; flowing arpeggios filled the huge room. I was consistently thankful that I had inherited some of my mother's piano prowess, even if I used it an environment far removed from her concertos and concert halls. We worked our way through the song. The levels of emotion were high, and the energy was fantastic. As we played the closing chords of the final chorus, Robbie belted out a high emotional last note, and it was over.

The applause was deafening. We hardly had time to catch our breath before Brooks bundled the band into a small bus and we headed back to our apartment block in the compound. Greatrex stayed at the stadium packing up, as did Kaitlin. I thought I would catch up with them both back at our quarters. It turned out I was wrong about that.

It was past midnight when I heard a vehicle roll up outside, followed by room doors opening and closing in the hallway. I went out to see Jack Greatrex walking toward my room. He looked tired.

"How'd it go?"

"No problem, all done," he replied.

"I want to catch up, but it may have to wait until the morning. I'd like to have a quiet word with Kaitlin tonight and see what's on her mind."

The Greatrex half-smile. "All work or a little play as well?"

I didn't have an answer to give him because I didn't know.

"Well, Kaitlin wasn't on the bus," Greatrex continued. "I assume she's coming back with Brooks."

"I'll wait," I said, surprised that I was feeling slightly miffed.

The next morning, I awoke around ten. A big show requires a fair bit of downtime to rebuild your energies. I had stayed up until around 2 a.m., but there had been no sign of Kaitlin or even Elliot Brooks for that matter. I went to sleep feeling even more miffed. Nicholas Sharp, just a jealous guy?

Around eleven the next morning there was a knock on the door; it was Greatrex. He walked in and sat down sluggishly on the couch. I offered him a coffee. We both started to wake up as the caffeine hit us.

"They want us to meet at the bus downstairs at one," he informed me. "Bring your clothes. Apparently, they'll provide us with dressing rooms and showers at the palace. We won't get back here until after the show. How'd it go with Kaitlin?"

"It didn't. I didn't see her," I explained. I left out the emotional details. Need to know basis.

"How'd you feel about that?"

Damn him.

"How about we take a stroll around the International Zone for an hour or so?" I suggested.

"Great idea, but they'll probably want to send someone with us … as protection."

We both chuckled. There was some humor in two former Marines requiring some nineteen-year-old army rookie to look after them. Oh well, it was the way of the world.

Twenty minutes later we were walking by the banks of the Tigris River, our military chaperone a few feet behind us, just out of earshot. The International Zone is the former Green Zone, an area of Baghdad where internationals were meant to feel safe and secure. It was well protected but not foolproof. It never had been.

We spoke about the possibilities of who Giles Winter's inside person may be; in the end we decided it could be anyone. We thought the most likely candidates were still Tommy Dabbs or Kaitlin Reed, mainly because they had joined the tour late. Also on our list was Elliot Brooks, mainly because we didn't like him. Apart from that, it could still be almost anyone in our touring group or even someone we hadn't met yet. I was pretty sure that we were lousy detectives. I was also decidedly uncomfortable with the idea that Kaitlin could be on the wrong side of this, but facts were facts and I couldn't discount them.

"When we get back to the embassy, I'm going to pull Kaitlin aside," I said. "I can't help but feel she has something she wants to tell me."

"I'll run interference with the ever-present Brooks," suggested Greatrex. "I'll make sure you get a few moments of quiet time together."

Perhaps a little light sarcasm there.

We returned to the embassy compound, dismissed our very patient bodyguard, and returned to our rooms to gather what we needed. Fifteen minutes later we were in the courtyard, with the rest of the touring group standing beside two buses that were due to take us to the Al-Faw Palace. No helicopter gunships needed for this trip, but there were armored vehicles in front and to the rear of the buses.

I'd looked around for Kaitlin but couldn't see her anywhere. I assumed she had gone to the palace early to begin arrangements. There seemed to be a bit of a kerfuffle among one group; I noticed both Robbie West and Elliot Brooks were among them. I thought it odd that Brooks was here, but Kaitlin wasn't. I then dismissed my observation as premature.

It wasn't.

Robbie came over to where Greatrex and I were standing with the rest of our band. He looked upset.

"What's wrong, Robbie?" asked Greatrex. "You look like you've lost your favorite guitar."

"It's not good. It's not good at all," said Robbie, not hysterical but clearly worried. "It's Kaitlin. No one has seen her or heard from her since last night—no one in the road crew, none of the entertainers, and none of our military friends. Her bed wasn't slept in. Kaitlin Reed has simply disappeared."

I looked at Greatrex. He looked at me. No words were needed. This changed everything.

Someone doesn't just disappear from within a US embassy without creating a substantial "situation." We were all told to return to our rooms and members of the Marine Corps Embassy Security Group would be along to interview each of us. The only concession they made to the fact we had a show to do was they agreed to interview the crew first, so they could then travel to the Al-Faw Palace and begin preparing for the performance. The people in charge had determined that the show would go on tonight. Too many dignitaries to disappoint. I also noticed that Marine guards were placed in every corridor of our apartment complex. Kaitlin's disappearance was being taken seriously.

I sat alone in my room while Greatrex was being interviewed. I was worried. Once I'd kicked myself a thousand times for not catching up with Kaitlin sooner, I began going through alternative scenarios in my head. Had someone arranged for Kaitlin to disappear? Had she found something out that she shouldn't have and made herself scarce to stay safe? Had she disappeared as part of Giles Winter's plan? Was she involved with his plan? This was all endlessly frustrating. I needed more facts. I realized I also needed to talk to Elliot Brooks; he was the last person seen with Kaitlin, and that brought him to the top of the suspect list. I had to be careful, however; you can't rough up a member of a respected organization like the USO just because you don't like them.

I was also aware that the security people would question Brooks very closely. They would suspect him for the same reasons I did. The difference was that they did not know the Giles Winter situation, which underscored this whole thing, and I couldn't tell them without endangering the lives of Leyla and Amira and possibly now Kaitlin. This was an extremely complicated mess.

Although the authorities were well resourced and extremely competent, the more I thought about it the more I realized there was a good chance it was going to fall to Jack Greatrex and me to sort through this maze. I didn't fancy our odds at all. We were getting in deeper and deeper in something way out of our league, and now another life may be at stake if things went wrong.

When my turn came, I was interviewed by a very sincere Marine security guard of around thirty years of age. Master Gunnery Sergeant Bernard Holstein seemed to take his job very seriously. I liked that. I told the gunny everything I knew about Kaitlin's movements. I told him I had worked with her before, and I told him Kaitlin was working closely with Brooks. I even told him of my military background. He seemed quite surprised at that and asked me why I left the Marines.

"Sorry, gunny, too complicated and not enough time," was my response. "Maybe over a beer one day." Nicholas Sharp avoiding hard questions.

Of course, I told Gunnery Sergeant Bernard Holstein nothing about Giles Winter, or the threat that was hanging over Greatrex and my heads. He should know, but he couldn't.

After the interview I gathered my things for the second time that day and went downstairs to board the bus for the palace. I felt a little guilty about holding things back from those investigating Kaitlin's disappearance, but I had no choice. I assumed Greatrex had done the same; he was already at the

Al-Faw Palace. The one thing I was certain of was that Elliot Brooks and I were going to have a long heart-to-heart tonight, whether he wanted to or not.

# Chapter 16

Surrounded by water on all sides, the Al-Faw Palace was an incredible building by anyone's standards. Built by Saddam Hussein, it was designed as a retreat for loyal members of Saddam's political party. As our convoy ventured across the causeway to the palace, I couldn't help but feel what a unique mixture of magnificent traditional Iraqi architecture and Saddam-style smoke and mirrors it was. It certainly cast an overpowering shadow over the artificial lakes surrounding it.

As we alighted from the bus, Brooks was there giving directions and instructions. There was, of course, no sign of Kaitlin. We all ventured inside and were directed to a large room where we were due to perform. I looked around at the enormous stone pillars surrounded by two levels of balconies under an ornately decorated domed roof. This would be a memorable venue.

We were being joined for this performance by the Britannia Royal Naval College Band for the more formal part of the evening's proceedings; it was a coalition event after all. In the back of my mind lurked the worry that Giles Winter appeared to have some sort of connection with someone in the British contingent. I let it go, for now.

I caught up with Greatrex. We checked over the gear and were then shown to our rooms for a shower and change. There wasn't much chance to talk, but that would come.

The formalities began with a small brass ensemble from the British band playing outside on the sprawling palace courtyard. The setting sun reflected a magical evening light over the waters. People of importance—some in uniform, some not—were scattered around in small groups. You wouldn't think there was a trouble in the world.

Greatrex and I stood with the other musicians in Robbie's band, taking in the sight of it all. I nudged him, and we moved away from the main group to have a quiet conversation. After comparing our separate interviews with the Marine embassy security and confirming we had each given the same story, we moved on to more pressing matters.

"We have to do something," I said. "We can't just let the Kaitlin thing go without trying to get a grasp on what's happening here."

"Agreed, but what?"

"For a start, I need to talk to Brooks. He was the last one seen with Kaitlin."

"All my antennas are telling me not to trust him, but we have no evidence that he's done anything wrong." Greatrex, the level-headed man.

"You're right, I know, but I still want to talk to him. It's time to break down a few walls."

"Breaking walls is okay, just don't break a person here. The last thing we need is to create a further incident." Greatrex was getting anxious.

"Point taken."

People were starting to move inside. As we caught up with

our group and followed them into the hall, I said to Greatrex, "Straight after the show tonight, a quiet but intense chat, that's all I want. Then we let things play out."

He nodded.

Inside, the formalities got underway. Everyone seemed to be telling each other what a great contribution they were all making to the peace and prosperity of the people of Iraq. I couldn't help but quietly muse to myself that I couldn't see too many of your average Iraqi people here tonight. Maybe politics is the same all over the world.

Following the speeches, our British colleagues performed. They were very polished and impressive. I appreciated any genre of music if it was played well.

The dignitaries ate at large circular tables placed around the room while a quartet of British musicians played jazz. I could hear them from our room backstage. A little later, as we were getting ready for our set, one of our crew members appeared at the door.

"Nicholas, there's a guy from the Naval College Band who says he'd like to have a word with you."

"Me? Sure, okay." I couldn't figure what a guy from the Naval band would want with me. I went into the corridor to find out.

"Nicholas Sharp?" It was a question more than a statement. The man before me was in full white dress uniform. He was tall, well built, looked to be in his midtwenties. I couldn't help but think of a younger, less weathered version of Daniel Craig.

"Yes, what can I do for you?"

He put out his hand. I shook it.

"Musician Stephen Beckley, first trombone, Britannia Royal Naval College Band."

"I enjoyed your performance, Stephen. Great band."

"Thank you, sir." He looked pleased. "I once performed with your mother, at the Royal Albert Hall. I was filling in with the London Philharmonic."

I was impressed.

"It was a wonderful performance. She truly is an amazing pianist."

"Thank you, Stephen. Very kind of you to say so." I was a little relieved that this was just turning out to be a visit from someone appreciative of my mother's work. I don't know what I expected. With all that was going on I was clearly living a bit too close to the edge.

Musician Beckley must have seen me relax, because the look on his face changed to one of concern.

"I'm sorry to do this to you, sir, but when one of the boys in our band told me you were here, I felt that I should talk to you."

"Is there a problem?"

"Well yes, sir, I think there might be. Of course, it may be nothing."

I looked up and down the ornate and massive corridor to make sure we weren't being overheard. Just precautionary.

"Go on."

"Well, last night, it was quite late, I couldn't sleep—you know, the heat and all that. We're billeted at the British embassy in the International Zone, so I thought I'd step out for a short stroll. I was walking down between two buildings when I heard some voices. I thought it was a bit unusual at two in the morning, I didn't say anything, but I did listen. Eavesdropped, I suppose."

Beckley hesitated, looking a little guilty.

"I would have done the same." Nicholas Sharp, encouraging.

"Well, I think I heard three voices: a Brit, an American, and an American woman."

Alarm bells started to ring in my head.

Beckley continued. "Well, it's probably nothing, but I heard your name mentioned, Mr. Sharp, and I also thought one of the men referred to the woman as Kaitlin."

The alarm bells turned into sirens.

"I wouldn't have thought that much of it except that when we arrived here, at the palace, this afternoon, someone mentioned that you were playing. Of course, I recognized the name because of the connection with your mother. The other thing was that everyone was talking about your tour manager going missing last night. It didn't bother me that much until I heard her name was Kaitlin."

I was standing there in stunned silence. Beckley took that as his cue to continue.

"I thought I just had to mention this to you, so here I am." He had finished.

I needed to know more.

"Did you hear much of what was being said?" I asked.

"Not really, things were pretty muffled. I heard one of the men saying, 'Keep away from Nicholas Sharp,' and someone mentioned that it was a 'dangerous situation.'"

I must have looked a little pale because Stephen Beckley's next words were, "Are you all right, Mr. Sharp?"

"Sorry," I mumbled, "just thinking. Was there anything else you heard, anything unusual or something that didn't seem to make sense?"

"Not really … oh yes, maybe."

"What was it, Stephen?"

"Well, I just thought it was odd that in the middle of a warm Iraqi summer, with everyone complaining about the heat, there was at least a couple of times they seemed to be talking about … well … 'winter.' Go figure."

"Go figure," I eventually responded. The word "winter" was reverberating around my head, again. My stomach felt tight and heavy, but I needed more.

"Now, Stephen, this may be quite important. At any stage did it seem to you that the woman you overheard as Kaitlin was being forced or coerced?"

"No, sir, I don't think so."

Damn. It seemed we had found Giles Winter's mole. Damn, damn, damn!

I must have let a couple of minutes' silence slip by in the corridor as a myriad of thoughts spun round in my mind.

"Are you sure you're all right, Mr. Sharp?"

Again, I found some words. "Yes, thank you, Stephen, and please call me Nicholas."

Stephen Beckley looked a little relieved that I had rejoined the world.

"I'll be going now, er, Nicholas. I just thought you would like to know what happened."

"Yes, thank you for being on the ball. Could I suggest you keep all this to yourself for now?"

Beckley looked unsure.

I went on, "That is unless you are specifically asked about it by a superior. I'm afraid I can't really explain why at this stage." That did the trick.

My new friend looked confused but reluctantly agreed.

"If you say so, sir."

Back to sir.

Stephen Beckley turned to leave.

"One more thing, Beckley." I decided to take a more authoritative tone because I needed his silence, at least for now. I was finding my feet.

"Yes, sir?"

"If you ever decide to give up being a musician, perhaps you could consider a career in intelligence."

I turned and went back into my room. I desperately needed to talk to Greatrex.

We were on stage within minutes after the conversation with Stephen Beckley. The show went smoothly, even if it was a bit of a blur to me. I had trouble concentrating on the music while I processed the information I had just received. It was not the kind of show a musician lived for anyway, at least not my kind of musician. Give me an enthusiastic, sweaty crowd over a bunch of stiffs any day.

Greatrex was at the side of the stage, as he usually was when I was playing. As we finished and walked off, he approached me.

"Okay, what's wrong?"

"You read me like the proverbial book," I hadn't had an opportunity to speak with him since the Beckley conversation. I pulled him aside backstage and filled him in.

"This puts a whole new perspective on the situation," he observed.

"It's glaringly obvious that Kaitlin Reed is Giles Winter's inside person," I responded. "I can't see it any other way."

He nodded.

"What about Brooks? Do we still talk to him?"

"Probably no need to stir up that hornet's nest for no purpose, at least not at this point," I said despondently.

Two hours later we were all back in our rooms at the US embassy. I was exhausted but couldn't sleep. More questions than answers were haunting my semiconscious state. How did Kaitlin Reed, a professional tour manager who I had known for some time, become involved in all of this? Why did she become involved? What was her relationship to Giles Winter? Why did she disappear? There was going to be no coming back from that. Any emotional thoughts I had about Kaitlin seemed to disappear into the ether. As I drifted off into a reluctant sleep, my conscious world gave me no answers; perhaps my subconscious would do better. My last thoughts were of an expression an old military buddy had once used to describe life in war-torn Baghdad. "It's all prayers and gunfire," he had said. That seemed to be my world now: "all prayers and gunfire."

# Chapter 17

We were all up early the next morning—early musician time, not military time. Our US Air Force helicopters were due to pick us up at ten for the flight to Camp Taji Joint Operations Base. As the first group, including Greatrex and myself, climbed aboard the now-familiar Pave Hawks, there appeared to be a heightened level of alertness among our military hosts. Whether it was that rocket attacks were still known to happen along our nineteen-mile route to Taji, or it was related to Kaitlin's disappearance, I was unsure.

The helicopter gunners scanned the ground below as we flew over the sea of low, flat brown rooftops interrupted only by the occasional higher, more modern structure. We looked down on the Tigris River. In the distance was last night's venue, the Al-Faw Palace. Below us the gigantic Swords of Qadisiyah appeared like the hands of a defiant giant rising out of the ground.

Before long, and fortunately without event, we saw the sea of runways, low-slung military buildings, and dry desert landscape that was the Camp Taji Base. Our pilots were experts, and we descended to a textbook landing. As per normal, Elliot Brooks was first on the ground and giving instructions. He may have been off our radar, but I still didn't like him. We were asked to group up in a bunch while the helicopters took off to pick up more of our team. Brooks then introduced us to Marine First Lieutenant Eric Lazlov. Lazlov was to oversee our security while we were on the base and he had a few things to say.

"Welcome to Camp Taj," he began. "We appreciate you coming all this way and hope you have an enjoyable stay with us. It is, of course, important that we keep you safe and secure while you are here. To that end, I must ask that you move around the base only in groups, and only with members of our security personnel accompanying you."

Lazlov scanned the group of us as he spoke. For a second his eyes seemed to halt on me, before moving on. I may have imagined it.

Lazlov continued, "You may be aware Taji is divided into two halves. The first of these is for coalition military personnel and coalition contractors, the other half is for the Iraqi forces we are assisting and advising. Please restrict your movements to the coalition side of the base."

We all got the picture.

Lazlov indicated a burly-looking Marine that was standing next to him. "Now Sergeant Bushby and his team will show you to your quarters. I will be around later to discuss arrangements for your performances."

Fifteen minutes later we were settled in our very simple military-style barracks, six to a room. This certainly wasn't the luxury of the US Embassy or the Al-Faw Palace, but we didn't care.

While some of the others went for a look around with their Marine minders in tow, Greatrex and I elected to stay behind.

"Well, clearly we can rule the embassy and the palace out as possible locations of the chemical weapon samples." We were past that point.

"So, it has to be here at Al Taji or the Al-Qa'im side trip." Greatrex responded.

"I don't see what we can do except wait until we're told what to do. What I don't understand is with Kaitlin out of the picture, who is our controller? Who has Winter organized to guide us to his stash?"

"I expect we'll find out soon enough," said Greatrex, masking his own impatience with the situation.

"Even then, we still have no plan," I responded.

"When have we ever had a plan that didn't change anyway?"

"Good point," I conceded, "We wait. I don't like it, but we wait."

An hour later the rest of our band had returned. We were just sitting around talking musician stuff when there was a knock on the door.

Elliot Brooks and Marine First Lieutenant Eric Lazlov walked in. Robbie West was with them.

Lazlov began, "We have made a small change to your itinerary, gentlemen. Mr. West here suggested I consult all of you. Although he is the leader of your band, he is of the belief any decision about movements here in Iraq should be agreed by all of you."

Greatrex and I looked at each other—another change to the itinerary.

"Now, a big consideration here is weather. The forecasters tell us winds are picking up in the area. You may not be aware that this region is frequently exposed to rather major sandstorms when conditions are like this."

Jack Greatrex and I had lived and worked through many

Iraqi sandstorms, but the others looked surprised.

"Accordingly," Lazlov continued, "we feel it would be better to get the Al-Qa'im side trip over and done with early, so you are not marooned by weather near the Syrian border. How does this sound to you?"

Robbie chimed in. "This all made sense to me, but I wanted to check with you guys first, particularly as Kaitlin isn't around to help with these decisions."

Brooks had said nothing until now.

"I don't see any alternative," he began. "Those troops at the forward base near Al-Qa'im are expecting you. The trip should proceed as soon as possible."

I noticed two things about what Brooks said. One was that he was very insistent that we go, the other was that he said "you" not "we." He was not coming with us. Even if he wasn't suspected as Winter's man anymore, something still felt a little wrong about him. I looked at Greatrex. His face seemed to echo my thoughts.

"If we go before the weather changes, are we sure we'll get back before the sandstorm hits?" I asked.

"Most likely," was Lazlov's simple response. "We should make it back in time."

We. I was starting to like this guy.

There was a bit of back-and-forth, but essentially, we all agreed to go early.

"Excellent," said Lazlov. "Now, a few points regarding logistics. You are aware that it is only you people in Mr. West's band that are going to Al-Qa'im. The only exception, civilian-wise, is Mr. Greatrex will go to be your tech and do your sound."

"You'll only use a small PA and basic instruments," said

Brooks.

"Everything including people and musical equipment must fit into two helicopters. No negotiation there, I'm afraid." Lazlov was definite.

Brian Pitt and Barry Flannigan looked decidedly nervous.

"Is this safe? Is there anything here to worry about?" asked Brian.

"Not really," replied Lazlov. "We send people up the border all the time. It is rare that there is an incident these days."

"Rare," repeated Barry. "Rare but not unheard of."

This didn't seem to reassure anyone. We all took a big breath.

"Are you still up for it? We did promise," Brooks playing the guilt card.

Robbie looked around the group; everyone slowly nodded.

"We're still up for it," he said to the lieutenant.

"Right," said Lazlov with the resolve of a military man who is decisive by nature, "we leave at 0900. That's nine in the morning, civilian time."

"We better sort out the gear," said Greatrex.

"We can pack the choppers tonight," instructed Lazlov. Deal done.

He and Brooks left the room.

"Robbie, is there any news regarding Kaitlin?" asked Barry Flannigan.

"Nothing," replied Robbie. She seems to have vanished off the planet."

I doubted that, but at that moment I doubted everything.

Greatrex moved up beside me, out of earshot of the others.

"This could be it," he said.

"It could," I answered, "or not." Nicholas Sharp sitting on the fence.

"One thing is for certain," I continued.

"What's that?" asked my friend.

"Nothing is certain."

# Chapter 18

At 0900 the following morning we climbed on board the two Pave Hawks sitting on the Tarmac at Al Taji. Although the band was getting used to traveling by chopper, no one seemed very relaxed about this journey. This wasn't helped by the fact that two US Air Force Apache gunships were on the tarmac next to the Pave Hawks, preparing to escort us.

Barry Flannigan looked at me skeptically as we walked toward our rides. As I was about to reassure him, he just looked at me and said, "I know, precautionary."

Nothing more to say.

We had packed light. Most of the group were in the first chopper with Robbie. Jack Greatrex and I were in the second aircraft with all the gear, carefully secured for flight.

Once aboard, we took off quickly. As I looked down, I saw Elliot Brooks' face staring up at us. I couldn't read his expression.

The Apaches stayed close. They were our protectors. There was no doubt now that the Air Force crew were very focused on the job at hand, their demeanor suggesting this was a bit more serious than the usual job of ferrying musicians and entertainers around. I looked across at Greatrex. This was something we had both done before; flying sniper teams into remote positions was not unusual in our former line of work. Next to Greatrex sat Lieutenant Lazlov. He was as good as his word and was here with us. His offsider, Sergeant Bushby, and a couple of others were in the lead Pave Hawk with the rest of the band. Next to me was a Marine who introduced himself as Lance Corporal Evan Taylor.

The flying time to Al-Qa'im was about an hour. Our route wasn't direct, as military wisdom suggested leaving plenty of space between us and any potential insurgent trouble spots.

There was not a lot of talk; the helicopter engines were loud, as was the sound of the wind. Everyone seemed to be concentrating on the landscape below, almost attempting to ensure a smooth and safe trip by willpower alone. The terrain started out flat, but as we approached Al-Qa'im steep foothills appeared in the desert landscape. It did not look very hospitable down there.

Finally, we landed at the forward base near Al-Qa'im without any trouble.

Once all the choppers had landed on the gravel landing area and the engines wound down, the whole band helped Greatrex unload the gear. Our Marine chaperones helped as well. The gear was taken by trucks to a small stage near the center of the base. Around ninety minutes later we were set up and ready to play. Although this was an acoustic set, we could still perform all of Robbie's hits; we just pared them down a bit to suit the instrumentation and production. A good song is a good song no matter how you present it.

It appeared that all the personnel who were able to leave their duties and come to hear us had done just that. The troops we played to all looked tired and a bit dusty. Their enthusiasm, however, was contagious, and we all got into the music pretty quickly. It turned out that our young Marine chaperone, Corporal Evan Taylor, was an enthusiastic amateur guitarist, so we got him up for a couple of songs. The crowd loved it, and it even put a smile on Lieutenant Lazlov's face as he watched over us. It was a great afternoon, and I got the impression everyone was just glad we'd made the effort to come all this way and provide them with a distraction from their daily duties and the tension of their environment.

Seventy minutes later, the show was over. Everyone seemed happy with it, and Robbie looked quite relieved. We all spent a little time chatting with the military folk. It was almost like we were all celebrities here, not just Robbie West.

Greatrex supervised the packing up of the equipment, and the Air Force and Marine personnel took it back to the helicopters for loading while we did the PR bit.

Throughout the afternoon Greatrex and I had kept glancing at each other to see if some contact had been made from one of Winter's people. There was nothing.

Late in the afternoon we climbed back on board our helicopters. Everyone went to the same aircraft they arrived in. Military order, but this time Jack Greatrex was sitting next to me and Lieutenant Lazlov and Corporal Taylor were sitting opposite.

As the undulating desert landscape fell away beneath us, I was certain I saw a look of contentment on Corporal Taylor's face; he had enjoyed his impromptu performance earlier, although now he was again focused on his role as our protector. His job, and that of all the other military personnel on board the two choppers, was to ensure that we, their guests, returned safely to Al Taji. They were all intent on making this so. I was doubly reassured by the now-familiar sight of the two Apache gunships shepherding us home.

Soon we were shooting along at around one hundred and twenty knots, flying at a very low altitude. The reasoning behind traveling so low was that we would only appear over the horizon at the last minute, giving any enemy little time to prepare an attack. Apparently, we were also taking a different route back to Taji. Unpredictability was an important defense strategy, no need to advertise our whereabouts.

Conversation was still too difficult in this noisy airborne environment, although we were wearing headphones that were patched into the helicopter's communications system. I leaned back against the seat, deep in thought. The fact that there had been no contact from Winter was confusing. I couldn't help but feel we were running out of time. On the positive side we were all safe and the most outwardly dangerous part of our tour had turned out to be uneventful.

Although I didn't know it at the time, within minutes I would realize that, by any and every definition of the term "uneventful," I could not have been more mistaken.

About fifteen minutes into the flight my thoughts were shattered by a sudden burst of static through the headphones. The voice from the pilot of the lead Apache came echoing through. "We have a visual of a possible insurgent group identified ahead, northeast ridge. It looks like they have a launcher of some sort. All craft, bank west now."

Then, "We have a SAM spike at three o'clock."

No sooner had we heard that than we heard a loud explosion ahead of us. We could see the Apache gunship in front of us seemingly shaking in midair and then spiraling down out of view. Plumes of smoke trailed from it.

It had all happened too fast.

"This is Apache One, we are hit, preparing for forced landing," came the pilot's urgent voice. Then there was another explosion, then nothing.

You don't get to be a Pave Hawk pilot in the US Air Force without having lightning reaction times, and our pilot went into immediate action. He banked sharply to the left and then began to reclaim some height.

At the same time, he gave urgent instructions to his copilot: "Dispense countermeasures."

Within two seconds flares were going off behind and below our machine.

The atmosphere within the cabin was electric, but it was frustrating that there was nothing any of us could do but trust our pilots.

The gunner on the lower side of the aircraft began putting down some intense fire, I assumed in the hope of deterring any more attacks.

All this happened over a period of about five seconds.

"Apache One down," came a voice over the comms. It was not the voice of the damaged Apache's pilot.

There were frantic interchanges between our pilot, the pilots of the remaining Apache, and the other Pave Hawk carrying the rest of the band.

"SAM spike at four o'clock—incoming, incoming." With an element of alarm I thought I recognized the voice as our pilot's. "Taking evasive action."

Not the words we wanted to hear.

Our helicopter seemed to roll at a ninety-degree angle to the ground. We all held on for our lives. Where a minute ago we were looking at sky and distant hills out the open doorway, now we were looking directly at the desert floor.

Seven seconds later, as we were all becoming a little hopeful, our world was quickly shattered. An incredibly loud explosion rocked our craft. My eyes closed involuntarily, but I could feel our chopper start to rotate. As I opened my eyes, I saw a bloody mess where our guitar-playing Corporal Evan Taylor had been sitting. Behind his prone body, a gaping hole in the side of the Pave Hawk exposed the desert and wind. Sitting next to Taylor was a badly injured Lieutenant Lazlov; his left arm looked completely mangled, and blood was seeping from his forehead.

Our pilot must have put us into an autorotation, which was sending us into some sort of controlled descent, but it was obvious, even to me, we were going down too fast, much too fast. The pilot seemed to push the nose forward, and our momentum picked up.

A second of hope.

"Prepare for a hard landing," came his voice over the headphones.

About five seconds later we hit the ground at way too high a speed; the whole aircraft seemed to stretch and implode at the same time. Every bone in my body felt as though it had been crushed. Among a blaze of noise and dust we eventually came to a halt.

Then there was silence.

# Chapter 19

As my senses returned, I looked around the damaged cabin. My first thought was for Jack Greatrex. He was still sitting next to me, conscious but stunned, a few cuts on his face, but other than that, thankfully all right. We had both been sitting on the protected side of the aircraft. I looked across at Evan Taylor. The young corporal was gone, there was no life left in his eyes. Next to him Lieutenant Lazlov was moaning and barely conscious. He would need some urgent medical attention. I seemed to be all right, but I was feeling very disorientated. Nothing broken, I thought. The gunner on the blast side of the chopper looked badly injured; blood flowed from a large wound in his side. He was unconscious. The gunner on our side of the craft seemed trapped by his massive gun. He, too, was only semiconscious.

Surprisingly, the aircraft's comms were still working. I picked up the headphones, which had flown off my head, and listened. There was no sound from our brave young pilot. I could make out the weakened voice of his copilot reporting to the other choppers.

"Hawk One down, the captain is unconscious, possibly worse. I'm trapped in here, no intel on our passengers."

We had no microphone on our headsets, so I couldn't inform

him, or anyone, as to our situation.

I heard the other Pave Hawk respond.

"We are clear, all civilian passengers on board are unharmed."

Thank God for that.

Their protector, Apache Two, responded.

"RTB, I'm going to escort you and your civilian cargo back to Taji. I will call for SAR to come in and retrieve personnel from the two downed ships. Coming out of Al-Qa'im they should be Delta fifteen away.

"Roger that." It was Pave Hawk Two responding.

I was relieved our bandmates were going to be all right; fifteen minutes was not long to wait for help.

I released my seat belt, then helped Greatrex release his. He took off his headphones and we clambered out of what was left of the aircraft.

We stood there for a couple of seconds, letting the events of the last few minutes sink in.

"You find the first aid kit and see what you can do for the lieutenant and the crew. I'm afraid there is nothing we can do for young Corporal Taylor."

It took a second for him to process my words.

I continued, "I'll check on the flight crew."

"On it," he responded. There was a sadness in his voice.

Greatrex went straight into action attending to our injured. I made my way around the front of the aircraft; my feet were unsteady, but at least I was able to move.

When I got to the front of the aircraft, I could see the copilot's description was accurate. There was a lot of damage on the pilot's side. I wasn't sure whether it was from the missile that attacked us or the landing. Our pilot was clearly unconscious; I went around to him and reached through the shattered window. I could feel no pulse.

I made my way back to the copilot. He seemed to be all right but was quite obviously trapped in his seat. It would take some cutting to get him out, and we didn't have the equipment to do it.

I knew help would be here soon.

At this point I sensed rather than felt a blast of moving air as a bullet struck the windshield of the helicopter. Then another. Unsurprisingly, the copilot looked extremely alarmed.

I called out to Greatrex. "Jack, enemy fire, rifle, coming from the northeast." The old job skills just kicked back in. I knew I had to draw the fire away from the front of the chopper, where the pilot was a sitting duck.

"Play dead," I said to him as I ran awkwardly to the rear of the machine. Greatrex joined me.

"Fifteen minutes just became a very long time," he observed. I nodded.

"If we do nothing, chances are in fifteen minutes most if not all of our group will be dead." I was just being realistic. "I presume they brought us down with a rocket grenade. If they have any more grenades there will be nothing left at all."

"What do you have in mind?" Greatrex asked.

I told him.

Less than five minutes later I was laying flat on my stomach, crawling behind a small hillock fifty yards to the rear of our Pave Hawk. In my hand was the M4 rifle that had belonged to Corporal Taylor. My plan had been simple. I would make my way some distance behind our chopper then head east and approach our attackers from the rear. It was a straightforward outflanking maneuver that I had performed many times as a

Scout Sniper. The big difference was that normally I would have had two or three hours to get into position; right now I had only a few minutes before Greatrex and I thought his distractions would be exposed as fraud.

Greatrex's job was to treat the wounded and make as much noise as possible at the rear of the aircraft to keep attention away from our trapped copilot. It turned out his name was Chief Warrant Officer Juan Santino. Santino was understandably nervous, but he saw the logic in playing dead in the front seat while Greatrex kept our observer's attentions elsewhere.

After the slow crawl away from the helicopter, I had to move into a crouched sort of run if I was to make the distance in time. It was nerve-racking, but fortunately the ground was undulating with some scattered trees. The trees and the hillocks allowed me cover. I was spurred on each time I heard one of the spasmodic gunshots being fired at our chopper. With each shot, I prayed the bullet had not found its mark.

Four minutes later, unobserved, I found myself again crawling over the rocks and sand to a rise that I thought may give me a view of our attackers. The sun was still hot, and I was bathed in sweat by the time I got to the top. I looked down and to the north. The first thing I saw was the Pave Hawk, around three hundred yards away. I scanned the landscape between me and the aircraft. Thirty seconds later I saw movement on a dune around 150 yards ahead of me and slightly to my right. Two figures were crouched low on a hillock, looking down at the chopper. From where I was, they looked like male Iraqis, but I couldn't be sure. What I was sure about was that one of the men carried a rifle, similar to the one I carried. The first thing that entered my mind was that if I could shoot him from here, then he could shoot me too. However, it was what lay between the two men that alarmed me the most. It was an old, probably Russian made, grenade launcher. Worse was that it appeared to be loaded and ready to fire. This weapon had the capability to finish off our chopper and everyone in or around it. It could also take out any aircraft sent to rescue us.

Too many lives at risk. I knew what needed to be done, and I knew I had to do it.

I began the process of getting into position. Lying flat, my forearm resting on the ground with the M4 butt resting snug against my shoulder, I looked down the length of the rifle barrel. The gun was pointing at the two men who were my target. I started to regulate my breathing; it was all about the breathing. Slow down, take control.

It was then that things suddenly started to go wrong, not around me, but in my head. Under the hot sun my thoughts appeared to seep into a baffling incoherence. I tried to focus, but I couldn't seem to manage it. I didn't need this now. This was no time for self-indulgence. Yet … I had sworn I would never return to this world. I had taken an innocent life, and I would not go back. I had said I would never again kill while hiding behind the camouflage of distance. Yet here I was. And what the hell was I doing here anyway, in Iraq, rifle in hand, taking aim at two people I didn't even know? I couldn't blame it on following orders. No one had given me any orders. I was now bathed in sweat and breathing too hard, which made it almost impossible to see clearly. Then the other side of my brain started working on me. You know what you have to do … Was that the voice of my father? Really?

I could feel the adrenaline. One hundred and fifty yards should be straightforward for a professional… but I wasn't a professional shooter anymore. I was a musician, creating not destroying, no longer making judgments, lethal judgments, on people's lives.

Then I thought about Jack Greatrex, the courageous young Warrant Officer Juan Santino, and the others on board that helicopter who were counting on me, trusting me to protect them. To keep them safe and alive.

I needed to act.

My hands were shaking. I aimed as carefully as I could, not much wind drift. I breathed out slowly, then pulled the trigger. One hundred and fifty yards ahead of me a puff of dust and rocks spat upwards next to one of the men. I had missed.

I think it was at that moment of surprise, anger, and frustration that the panic left me. A wave of clarity and calmness replaced it. I took aim again. The man on the left was turning around. I breathed out slowly again and fired, straight into the side of his head. His companion grabbed for a rifle I hadn't seen and swung around toward me. I pulled my trigger again, he went down clutching his chest. He wouldn't be getting up.

I slumped in a heap, exhausted, deflated. I felt overemotional and emotionless at the same time. Was that possible? Nicholas Sharp, more conflicted than you could imagine.

But I had done the job. I had protected.

Then I threw up.

# Chapter 20

Fifteen minutes later, after a shaky walk back to the Pave Hawk, during which I constantly checked for other insurgents in the hills, I made it back. There were no additional wounded, thank God. Greatrex looked relieved to see me. I was certainly relieved to see him.

In the distance we heard the search and rescue helicopters coming in from the west. Two minutes later, two Apache gunships circled above us. Juan Santino had radioed that our attackers had been taken out, but the Apache pilots were being careful. After what we had just been through, I didn't blame them. Two minutes after that, two new Pave Hawks came into view. The Apaches continued to circle overhead while the Pave Hawks landed near us in two huge clouds of dust. Medical personnel jumped out of one chopper while armed Marines vaulted out of the other. Within ninety seconds everyone had taken up positions either attending the wounded or guarding the crash site perimeter.

Jack Greatrex and I watched with relief when the injured were stretchered into the medevac aircraft. In isolated sadness we then watched the bodies of Corporal Evan Taylor and our courageous pilot loaded aboard.

A very intense-looking Marine officer came forward and

introduced himself as Major Grant Jacobs. He asked us to describe the events of the last hour or so.

We did.

The look on Jacobs' face when we finished was almost total disbelief.

"And you are a musician, Mr. Sharp? And Mr. Greatrex here is your technical support? Is that correct?"

We both nodded. I couldn't help but feel like a naughty schoolboy in the principal's office.

Jacobs shook his head. "Well, that's one to tell the grandkids, although they probably wouldn't believe me." He gave us a perplexed look and said, "Somehow I think there may be a bit more to this, and to the two of you."

Smart man, that Major Jacobs.

A lance corporal approached Jacobs. "Time to go, sir."

"We'll talk a little more later, gentleman. For now let's get you back to Camp Taji."

With that, we all climbed aboard the helicopter the Marines had arrived on. Most of the Marines were staying on to begin the retrieval of the aircraft, essential military equipment and our musical gear, if it had survived.

Five minutes later our chopper was following the medevac aircraft toward Taji. One of the Apaches was escorting us, the other was remaining on guard duty at the crash site.

Twilight was setting in; it brought a certain transparent beauty to the desert as we looked down across the landscape. I thought of the men who had died today. Sadly, that count now included the confirmed deaths of the crew of our guardian Apache that had gone down. They had probably saved our lives in the process.

Then I thought back to what had happened as I lay on that

hill overlooking the helicopter and the insurgent attackers. I thought about the rifle that I had held in my hands, and the wrestling match I had endured with the ghosts of a past life.

Enough. It was time for this day to end. I needed it to.

When we landed at Taji we were greeted by Elliot Brooks waiting on the floodlit tarmac.

"We are all so relieved that you two are all right," he said, looking at Greatrex and me.

"Tragically, there are several people who are not all right, Elliot," I responded briskly. "I think we should cancel the rest of the tour and head home now."

"Let's not be too hasty. There are a lot of people counting on your work here. Get a good night's sleep and we'll talk tomorrow." Elliot Brook's empathy was underwhelming.

The mood on the base appeared to be somber as we made our way to our barracks. Word had got out. Losing fellow servicemen and women hurt, no matter the circumstances.

By the time we reached our quarters, Jack Greatrex and I were exhausted; the day had beaten us. All we wanted to do was collapse into our bunks and sleep until we were done. As we opened the door Robbie West and the rest of the band were there to greet us. The relief that spread over their faces was palatable—warm and sincere.

"My God," said Robbie. "I never thought I'd be so glad to see a damn piano player." He then threw his arms around both of us. The rest of the band joined in.

"We saw you go down as we made a beeline for home," said Brian. "We didn't believe anyone could live through that crash."

"Sadly, not everyone did," said Greatrex.

We told them about Evan Taylor and the pilot.

Sadness enveloped the room. We all thought of that young man, guitar in hand, joining us on stage. Had it only been a few hours ago?

"Well, that's horrible, but you are here and that is fantastic." Robbie, always upbeat.

"We heard some stories … stories about how the insurgents that shot you down were killed." It was Barry Flannigan, too wise for his own good.

"They said you were involved, Nick." Robbie eyed me suspiciously.

"We heard that it was the two of you who saved those lives today." Brian, sounding foolishly in awe.

"That couldn't be right, could it?" asked Barry.

I looked at Greatrex. He shrugged his shoulders.

"Sit down, boys," I said. "It's time we had a little talk."

And we did.

# Chapter 21

Things always looked different in the morning light. With a restless but much-needed sleep behind us, Greatrex and I felt back on our game. We hadn't had a chance to sit down and debrief yet; hopefully, that would come later today.

At eleven we met in the mess hall with the entire touring party. This included all the performers, the crew, and Elliot Brooks. Major Jacobs was in one corner, watching over us, or watching us; I wasn't sure which. The consensus was that the tour should continue. This was certainly the line Brooks was pushing. Despite that, people didn't like the idea of terrorists sending us packing, and I couldn't help but respect their attitude. Robbie's group was given the option of leaving. Everyone felt that we had been through enough and had earned the right to go home. Had it been the night before, I would have said "thanks" and hit the first C-130 out of there. It was now the next morning, and after a brief talk we the foolhardy, Robbie's bandmates, had decided to stay. We only had one more show to do before heading off to England anyway. We were not going to be run out of town. Underlying that sentiment was the need for Greatrex and I to stay. Like it or not, we had a job to do. Although yesterday put a lot of recent problems out of our minds, today we were acutely aware of Leyla and Amira still being held hostage, counting on us to get them out.

I also had some thinking to do. Those few minutes on the hill overlooking the insurgents and the helicopter had shaken me. It was becoming painfully obvious that I had some baggage to sort.

The show at Camp Taji was going to be a big one. It was a big set-up with a large stage, scaffolding, and lighting towers. It would be a whole day to rig the stage before anyone put any sound system or instruments up there. The audience should be around two thousand, including the military personnel, the Iraqi troops, and contractors from the coalition countries. Security would be tight. There had been some incidents between Iraqi troops and coalition personnel. This concert was an event of goodwill, so no one wanted to take any chances with an insurgent-driven episode, especially after our attack.

The plan was for military personnel to start assembling the stage right away. The following day, weather permitting, the musical equipment would go up and the concert would be that night. Weather could be an important component. Brooks had briefed us that the forecasters predicted a worsening of the winds; we could already see signs that something was brewing.

He had also told us that Lieutenant Lazlov and the crewmen of our helicopter were expected to make a full recovery. That was great news.

That afternoon Greatrex and I had a chance to talk in private for the first time since the chopper attack. We walked around the base with a couple of our Marine minders trailing a few steps behind. The minders were now under the charge of a very focused Sergeant Bushby. If I didn't know better, I'd say that he and his men were showing us an increased level of respect. I suppose troops talk.

"How are you feeling, my friend?" I asked Greatrex.

"Tired, stiff, sore, and pissed off." Straight to the point. "How about you?"

"Pretty much the same," I responded. "A day like yesterday was not in my plans at all, nor will it be ever again."

"What was that John Lennon quote you're always saying? Life's what happens while you're …"

"Shut up," I interrupted, but smiling at the same time.

"Shutting up, sir." Self-amusing sarcasm.

We wandered toward the area of the base where the concert would take place. We wanted to check it out.

"So even after all the tragedy and adventure of yesterday, we are no closer to where we need to be," I said.

"We will be soon," said Greatrex. "Law of averages; we're running out of time and opportunity."

He was right.

We rounded a corner at the end of a row of barracks to face a large, empty space. It was a gathering area for dust and gravel surrounded by a sea of low-slung military buildings. At one end a large stage was being assembled on some serious scaffolding. When military engineers build something, they really build it.

We walked toward the stage.

"First things first," I said. "I've been thinking it through. I don't figure that yesterday's attack had anything to do with Giles Winter; there would have been no point."

"Agreed," said Greatrex.

"So, moving on, if you were Winter's man, or woman, and you wanted us to find something on this base, but you didn't

want anyone to see us finding it, what would be your timing?"
I was trying to get ahead of this thing.

Greatrex thought for a moment. "The best time not to see
something is when you can't see."

"Thanks, Yoda," I replied with my own sarcasm, but I thought
I saw where he was going with this. "The weather?" I
suggested.

"The weather," he replied. "If this turns out to be as bad a
sandstorm as everyone is predicting, it would be like having
the place to ourselves out there."

"Only if we can find our way around." After the last twenty-
four hours, my already flagging optimism was all but gone.

"Besides," I went on, "how could Winter have predicted a
sandstorm?"

"You can accuse Giles Winter of many things," said my friend,
"but you can't accuse him of failing to be an opportunist."

"Yeah." My voice sounded weary, even to me. "He just keeps
making the most of every situation that rolls his way, and they
just seem to keep on rolling."

There were a couple of moments' silence between us as we
watched the team erecting the big stage in front of us.

"There's one thing that still bothers me." Not a lot of things
bother Greatrex, so I was listening. He went on, "The coalition
forces knew that Al Taji was a base for Saddam's production
of chemical weapons and nerve agents. They went over the
base and the general area with a fine-tooth comb. How are
we meant to find something the experts missed?"

I looked at my friend. He looked as weary as he sounded.

"I've been thinking about that, too, and I reckon there are
two key factors at play," I said. "Number one is that the
coalition experts were looking for stockpiles of chemical

weapons. You and I now know that Winter's "network" arranged for them to be destroyed before the coalition forces moved in. They were looking for large amounts of the materials in places you could store large amounts. We are looking for a small package of samples and formulas in a place you could keep a small package. A small package is much easier to hide."

"I'm impressed by the great man's logic, considering his current state of mind." Greatrex was clearly having a mildly sarcastic day. "Now what about factor number two?" he asked.

"That one is easy," I said. "We are going to know exactly where to look; Winter is going to tell us."

I felt quite pleased with myself, and Jack Greatrex looked impressed. I was on a roll, so I couldn't stop now.

"Besides," I continued. "I know where they are."

Greatrex's jaw seemed to drop. His mouth was going to let in a hundred desert flies.

"You what?"

"I know where they are. Well, at least I think I do."

"Mr. Sharp and Mr. Greatrex, how nice to see you." It was the voice of the very persistent Major Jacobs. "I was hoping we could catch up."

"Hello, major," I said. Greatrex nodded. Why did I feel we were about to have the "further little talk" that we were promised yesterday at the crash site?

"I hope you have both recovered from yesterday's ordeal. It must have been very tough for a couple of civilian musician types."

We both nodded.

"But perhaps not so tough for a couple of former Marines, including a sniper with a more than outstanding track record."

As ever, I looked to Greatrex for a cue. As ever, he shrugged.

"I think you've been going through some personnel files, major." I said.

"I have."

My turn to shrug. "Okay, major, let's talk." For the second time in twenty-four hours, Nicholas Sharp, *This is Your Life*.

Greatrex and I explained as much as we reasonably could to Major Jacobs, but it wasn't much. Just background, really. There was, of course, a lot more we couldn't explain to him, including everything about Giles Winter and the weapon samples. After we finished, he paused.

"So, it is just coincidence that you two are in Iraq as part of this USO tour. There is nothing more at play here?"

I can shoot, I can play piano, I can talk, and I can even fight, but the one thing I always have trouble with is a straight-out lie. So I found something interesting to look at on the ground. Greatrex must have found the something interesting too.

"I thought so," continued Jacobs. "Nothing more you would care to enlighten me about?"

The ground was still interesting. I felt bad; for some reason I felt all right about this man. I wanted to trust him, but I didn't have much trust left in me.

"I thought not." Jacobs was winding up. "Based on your actions yesterday, and what I read in your military files, you two are men to be trusted. The problem is I am not very trusting. Not taking people and events at face value is an occupational trait."

I could relate to that.

"Gentlemen, consider yourselves on a very short leash. I do not want unnecessary trouble here under my watch."

He turned and began to walk off. I wasn't sure what was

worse, that we couldn't or wouldn't confide in him or that he was being so fair with us. As soon as the major was out of earshot I looked to Greatrex for support.

"We could use some help and local knowledge," he said quietly. "There is no one else."

"Can we trust him?" That was the million-dollar question. "I don't need to remind you what is at stake here."

"Take a Yoda moment. What is your gut telling you about this man?" asked Greatrex.

I looked up at Major Grant Jacobs, ten yards distant and walking away, his back to us.

"Ah, major, do you have a couple more minutes?"

He stopped and turned toward us.

"There may be a couple of small points we left out," I continued.

A small, welcoming smile appeared on the major's face as he strode back toward us.

"Of course," he said. "I'm all ears."

I began. Greatrex joined in and filled in details at the appropriate times. For better or worse we told Major Grant Jacobs about Giles Winter, about Leyla and Amira ... about everything.

Twenty minutes later, standing in the middle of that square, I felt a sense of relief. It may have been the exaggerated aftereffects of yesterday's traumas, but I knew we had been feeling the weight of keeping all this information to ourselves for too long. By talking to Jacobs, we knew we had no answers, but at least we had another head looking at the situation from all angles, maybe fresh angles. Jacobs also knew his way around the very complicated international politics and people that make up Taji Base.

The major was at first speechless, almost as if trying to decide whether to believe our wild story. Then, as if making his decision, "You two appear to have an impossible task: your friends die or many more people are put at risk."

"That had occurred to us," Greatrex replied.

"Our only hope, and it is faint, is to try and get ahead of this thing and outplay Winter, but he is a smart man. So far, we have had little success," I ventured.

"You mentioned you thought you knew where the samples may be. Can you share this information?"

"I wouldn't mind hearing an answer to that question myself," said Greatrex.

I shrugged—more of a sag, really. I almost wished I hadn't shot my mouth off about this. Too late now.

"Well, it's more of a theory than a statement of fact," I began.

"Please continue." The Greatrex half-smile again.

"Okay, well, it seems to me that when the coalition forces invaded Iraq and took control in Operation Iraqi Freedom there were several important factors; these included the obvious military aspect of making ground and getting rid of Saddam, but there was more to it."

I could see I had their attention.

"We had to persuade the Iraqi people that we were the good guys, win their hearts and minds, as they say. Part of this was making sure we minimized any cultural offense that we caused their people."

"Yes, correct, of course, but how does this help us locate samples of chemical weapons and nerve agents?" A fair question from Greatrex.

"Well, the one thing we couldn't afford to do was disrespect the Iraqi people's religious beliefs. If we did that, we would never be forgiven, and we may as well have gone home."

"So, you think the hiding place for these samples has some religious connotation?" Jacobs was proving to be a very smart man, and I hoped, a good ally.

"Right."

"Saddam Hussein believed in Sunni Islam, at least outwardly, because that was his powerbase," observed Greatrex.

"Correct," I continued. "So it occurred to me that the safest place to store a small package of formulas, nerve agents, and chemical weapons would be under some sort of religious sanctuary."

"You mean a religious figure would have them?" asked the major.

"No, people come and go, especially in times of conflict. What I mean is I believe that the package is on this base, in or under a building that has been used for religious purposes. It would be a building the coalition investigators would be reluctant to demolish or invade out of religious respect."

"It would also be small enough not to be investigated as a storage location for larger amounts of chemical weapons," added Greatrex.

Now we were on a roll.

Greatrex and I looked to the major—local knowledge required.

"Do you have any ideas?" I asked him.

Considering it was less than an hour ago that Major Jacobs had no knowledge of the situation at all, he seemed to be rising to the occasion, if still a bit reluctantly, as a true professional would.

"I have a few possibilities. Give me two hours to look into it, and I will get back to you." Confidence.

I was satisfied with that. Jacobs turned to go.

"Oh, by the way," he continued, "I nearly forgot, I have a message for you. It came through to our comms center while you were at Al-Qa'im." The major reached into his pocket, produced a folded piece of paper, and passed it to me.

It read, "Call me as soon as you can. It may be important." It was signed Kenny M. Kenny Medina.

I passed it to Greatrex. Although this was a bit surprising, I knew immediately that I needed to contact Kenny ASAP. I also knew civilian communication was very limited in Iraq.

"Major, one more request before you go." Again, Major Jacobs stopped mid-stride. "Can I use your communications center to contact someone in LA? It could be important."

"In normal circumstances that wouldn't be a problem," he responded. "Sadly, we are currently in 'River City' due to the deaths of the servicemen on your sojourn yesterday."

"River City" was the military code word for "reduced communications." In the modern days of the internet and social media it meant that communication with home was cut off for all personnel except for essential operational matters. Cases had occurred where families of servicemen killed in the theater of war had found out from wives of their colleagues about the death of their loved ones before qualified military support personnel were able to get to them. In one case a wife had found out about her husband's death on Facebook. The "River City" blackout gave the military support system time to swing into action.

"Understood," said Greatrex. We both knew about the blackout policy.

"How incredibly convenient for Giles Winter," I said. "Once again, the opportunist is given a free pass." Damn!

# Chapter 22

It was early afternoon by the time Greatrex and I made it back to our barracks. We were not allowing ourselves a lot of hope of sorting this mess, but at least we had another ally on board. Risky as it was, we hoped Major Grant Jacobs could be helpful. We knew we were facing a very uncertain next twenty-four hours.

As we walked into our building, we found it in chaos. People were running everywhere, sorting gear and instruments. It seemed to be a state of panic.

"What's going on?" I asked Barry Flannigan.

"Elliot Brooks was just here. It seems winds are going to go crazy from about 1 a.m. and continue through the following day and night. They've decided to bring the concert forward twenty-four hours. The show will be tonight."

"Tonight. Can we get it set up in time?" I asked no one in particular.

"They are bringing in extra military riggers to help," Brain Pitt responded. "They reckon they can have us on stage by seven-thirty."

"Shit, I haven't even checked any of the gear that was in the crash yesterday," said Greatrex. "That includes your Nord piano."

He didn't need to remind me that was the keyboard with our "special compartment."

"I'll see to it now." And he was off.

The rest of the afternoon became a model of frantic organization and disorganization as crew, military, and musicians worked frantically to make the show happen in time. I joined them.

By four, the stage was built, and the crew were setting up the lights, PA, and stage gear. By six we were ready to go. Unbelievable.

Brooks addressed our pre-show briefing in the mess hall at six-fifteen. "Well, we've done it folks; we're ready to rock, literally." A round of applause.

I thought about the cultural gap between the military and the music industry that I had worried about earlier in the tour. When a job needed to be done, there was no gap.

"We've managed to get word out regarding the change in time; there are some advantages of existing in a relatively small community," he continued. "People are starting to arrive already. The show starts at 7.30 p.m. and should be over by ten. Our crew and the army riggers will pull everything except the stage down as soon as you finish. We should be clear by midnight, a good hour before the sandstorm hits."

"What about the gear that was in the helicopter crash?" It was Brian.

"We've salvaged enough to make the show work tonight."

Greatrex looked over at me. He had already told me that my keyboards were all right.

The buzz began to grow. This was one of the biggest shows of the tour, and everyone was getting excited.

"One more thing." It was Brooks again. "After the show,

everyone is expected to go straight back to their rooms. The sandstorm will certainly last the rest of the night and possibly most of the next day. These storms can be violent. We don't want to lose anyone."

Brooks seemed to have a short memory. I thought of those we had lost on this tour already. I didn't want to lose anyone else.

Several hours later I was standing at the side of the stage with the rest of the band, waiting to go on. I looked out to a sea of expectant faces. Again, the enthusiasm was high. It was well and truly dark, but lights from the scaffold towers lit the space. A few hours ago, this felt like a parade ground; now it felt like an arena.

Greatrex was making the final adjustments to my keyboards. He and I had arranged to catch up with Major Jacobs straight after the show. The major had let us know he had some information for us, but in all the hectic preparations with the change of show times, we hadn't been able to meet. We had to prioritize the show over the meeting because we knew we were being watched. We still didn't know by whom.

I noticed that the wind was picking up, but nothing to worry about yet.

I felt a tap on my shoulder. Turning around I immediately recognized the smiling face of Chief Warrant Officer Juan Santino, our Pave Hawk copilot. He put his hand out to shake. I took it but hugged him as well. Not very military-like.

"I just wanted to say thank you, Mr. Sharp. Without you and Mr. Greatrex doing what you did, well, we would have been in deep trouble out there yesterday."

"You're a brave man, Juan," I responded. "You kept your cool under extreme pressure. I think we had the easy job."

145

"Anyway, I just wanted to say thanks. If there is anything I can ever do—"

I didn't let him finish. "What you can do for me is have a great life. We all got a second chance yesterday, or at least most of us did." I paused. "Make the most of what's ahead."

"Ladies and gentlemen," came the announcement over the speakers, "please welcome the Robbie West Band."

"Better go," I said. We shook hands again before I turned toward the stage. I was feeling quite emotional, and a little inspired. Time to let the magic happen.

From the first chord of the first song, the crowd went wild. They were screaming, dancing, and singing along. What a way to earn a living. I looked out on the floodlit arena. Now I was on stage, I had a much better view of who made up our audience. There were coalition military personnel, of course, but also many people out of uniform. I presumed these to be civilian contractors, brave people to come here for work. What really stood out to me were the Iraqi troops standing alongside our own. They seemed to be enjoying themselves just as much as our people. It never ceased to amaze me—the powerful hold music has on humanity. Differences seemed to be cast aside. I was proud to be part of a night like this; it was just special. Truth be known, this was just what we all needed right now.

Robbie was in his usual fine form, making friends and winning hearts. Everyone seemed to know all his songs. They sang along with heartfelt voices to the ballads, danced to the up-tempo rock tunes, and joined Robbie in every chorus through the set. By halfway through the show we were all bathed in sweat, working hard, and loving every second of it. It was, however, a little gut-wrenching when we played one of the songs that young Corporal Evan Taylor had played with us the day before. Forevermore, this would be his song. We talked about not including it because it could be hard emotionally. We had, though, been told we couldn't dedicate a song to Evan until the communication ban was over, so we played his song with his memory in our hearts. I don't think there was a musician on stage without a tear in their eye. Music as therapy.

We started the final song. It was the same one we ended the show with at the US embassy. Was that only a couple of days ago? So much had happened since then. Again, I started with resounding chords on the piano before the rest of the band joined me. Way too soon, Robbie was hitting his final notes, as powerful as ever.

I didn't want this to be over. I didn't want it to be over because the atmosphere was uplifting. I didn't want it to be over because this is what I do. I also didn't want this to be over because as the winds picked up, I felt they were not only heralding the arrival of a colossal sand storm; I feared they were also ushering in a dangerous and disturbing night for Jack Greatrex and me.

It's an ill wind ...

# Chapter 23

It was almost midnight. Jack Greatrex, Major Grant Jacobs, and I were sitting in the major's office. Greatrex and I were perched on chairs either side of his desk. The show had been packed up in record time, which was just as well because we could hear the winds increasing as they violently whipped sand into the buildings outside. Greatrex and I had gone back to our quarters after the show, as instructed. We hadn't stayed there very long. By now our fellow musicians were getting a little used to our "extra-curricular" activities and didn't hesitate to agree to cover for us if anyone came knocking. Not that anyone would in these conditions.

"I have some ideas as to the location you are looking for, gentlemen. According to your hypothesis, Mr. Sharp, it could be one of four locations …"

I interrupted the major.

"I know which one," I said confidently.

"But you haven't even looked at the alternatives yet." The major was becoming a little irritated with me.

"I don't need to," I said. I then produced a piece of paper from my pocket and put it on the desk. The other two stared at a series of figures on the paper.

"GPS coordinates," observed the major.

"Where and when did you get these?" asked Greatrex, a more than fair question.

"Well, there's the thing," I said. "We were expecting a tap on the shoulder, a word from Winter's man. What we got was an envelope stuck inside the door of my locker in our room. I found it after the show. I hadn't had a chance to tell you yet."

"Well, there you go. Now we know," said Greatrex, maybe a little miffed.

"We will in a minute," said Major Jacobs. He was calling up a satellite search program on his computer. He input the coordinates from the paper. "Got it," he said, as he moved his laptop so we could all see the screen.

We looked on as the major explained.

"This is one of the possibilities I had on my list." He seemed a tiny bit pleased with himself.

"What is it exactly?" I asked. "And where is it within the camp?"

"It's a disused building on the Iraqi side of camp. It was once a mosque. A much larger mosque has since been built on the other side of the Iraqi section of the base, so this building is no longer used. At least not for prayer." Jacobs pointed to the coordinates on the paper. "It appears your theory was correct, Mr. Sharp."

"What is the building used for now?" asked Greatrex.

"I'm not totally certain, but I think only for storage purposes."

"Will it be difficult for us to get into the Iraqi section of the camp?" My turn for a question.

"Normally, security is very tight between the two sections. Tonight's concert was an exception. It would normally be unusual for visitors such as yourselves to be allowed in that area."

"Unusual, but not out of the question?" asked Greatrex.

"Tonight," the major continued, "tonight I think nothing is out of the question. Listen."

We all listened. We certainly didn't listen in silence. As we had been talking, the racket outside had been growing louder. It was now overpowering.

"If you are foolish enough to go out in that sandstorm, then you could probably get just about anywhere on this base unseen. A pair of bolt cutters would need to be your keys." The major had finished.

"We are foolish enough," I said. Greatrex nodded and grinned.

"How do we know where the package will be once we find the building? It could take hours to search, hours we don't have."

My friend had a point. I had an answer. I reached across the desk and turned the piece of paper over. On the other side, one word was written: "beneath." That was all.

"There you go," said Greatrex. "Maybe we bring a shovel."

"I'm not so sure. I have a feeling once we get there, we'll know what the package is beneath, or at least we'll figure it out," I said confidently.

"Well, your intuition has been pretty good so far; let's go with that," said the major. I appreciated the faith.

I looked across at the big fella. "Let's get to work," I said, and began to get up.

"Gentlemen, please, it is hard enough to find your way around this base in normal conditions. Out there tonight you will have no chance on your own."

Greatrex and I looked at each other again. Major Jacobs

probably had a good point.

He continued, "I also am feeling a little foolish this evening. I will be your guide."

I was going to argue with him, but he was right; we needed him.

"Thank you," I said, and meant it.

I turned to Greatrex and said, "Local knowledge."

"I also think you may be underestimating what conditions are like out there. You will need these."

Major Jacobs walked over to a large cupboard, opened the door, and reached in. He produced some heavy robes and scarves. They looked as though they had belonged to local Iraqis.

"As well as protection, these will also provide an element of disguise if anyone sees us."

He also produced three flashlights.

"These will be of little use outside, but they may help inside the building."

Local knowledge and wisdom. I was beginning to feel a little optimism, just a bit.

We got up and put on the major's garments. If I had a mirror, I wouldn't have recognized myself.

We then took a deep breath and headed out the door into the night.

It was like running into a concrete wall. We were immediately pounded with tens of thousands of particles of sand. They felt like bullets and I could feel them stinging through my thick clothing. In an instant the small part of my face that was exposed felt like someone had taken to it with a knife. Greatrex and I had been caught in sandstorms before, but never anything like this.

Through squinted eyes, I looked ahead and could see almost nothing. After a minute or so I could only just make out the two figures ahead of me. I knew them to be Greatrex and the major, but visibility was so bad I couldn't identify who was who. I was reminded of the film *Ice Station Zebra*, where the plots twists take place in a blinding snowstorm on an ice cap. I would have swapped that ice cap for this sandstorm in an instant.

One of the two figures led the way; I assumed it to be Major Jacobs. We seemed to go on forever, moving between endless rows of buildings. They must have offered some protection from the storm, but we didn't notice it. We did, however, notice it when we left the narrow laneways and had to cross a large open space. I assumed it to be the area where the concert was held just a few hours before, but all I could see now was sand and darkness, so I couldn't be sure. The moment we left the protection of the buildings, misery became torture. The wind was so strong that standing was difficult. Missiles of sand pulverized us, and moving forward was almost impossible. As we slowly edged our way across the space, I found it harder and harder to breathe. I just focused on the shadow ahead of me and hoped for the best. Stopping or collapsing out here would almost certainly mean a prolonged and painful death.

After what seemed like an eternity, we had crossed the space and had again found the limited protection of some more buildings. I would never complain about wind and rain, or any weather for that matter, ever again. A couple more twists and turns and we found ourselves blocked by a tall wire fence. We couldn't see the top of it, but Major Jacobs had told us that razor wire ran the length of it. As we huddled there, the wind's shriek was still so loud we couldn't begin a conversation.

Always prepared, the major produced a small pair of bolt cutters out of his robes and began to cut. As I looked over his shoulder, back toward the way we had come, I thought for a fleeting second I saw the shadow of a figure move behind one of the buildings. Not possible, I thought. I couldn't be certain of seeing anything in this weather.

A few minutes later we were through the fence. There were no signs of any guards or personnel. Why would there be in conditions like this? A couple of times I glanced behind us, but my imaginary friend didn't reappear.

I had heard that the Iraqi section of the camp, where we now found ourselves, was not as well provisioned as the coalition side. As we began moving between buildings, I could see no evidence of this, probably because I could see no evidence of anything. My body felt numb with pain, and my eyes stung as though they'd been attacked by hornets, but it was my breathing that was beating me. I just couldn't find clear air to get into my lungs. I was right at the point of tapping Greatrex on the shoulder to say I could go no further when the major pointed to a small stone building just ahead of us. I couldn't hear what he was saying, but from his mannerisms I thought this may be our former mosque; at least I hoped so.

I couldn't see much of the outside of the structure, but it looked primitive and basic. It had a very solid-looking wooden door that was bolted shut. There was a large padlock attached to the bolt. It looked too big for the major's bolt cutters. I thought we might have come all this way, through all this pain, for nothing. Despair turned to hope when the major produced a small pointed screwdriver from his robes and proceeded to work the lock. He had it open in three painful minutes. A resourceful man, our major. We opened the door;

no one would hear us over the sound of the wind. I shone my flashlight briefly around the inside wall of the building. There was no sign of movement, so we entered the darkened room.

I closed the door behind us. Although we could still hear the storm outside, it felt like silence in the relative shelter of the room. The three of us took a few moments to catch our respective breaths. Greatrex felt around the wall for a light switch. He found it and flicked it on. Nothing.

"That was a life experience I would not care to repeat," I announced as I taught myself how to breathe again.

"A little bad news there; we're going to have to find our way back, you know." Greatrex bringing me back to reality. Thanks so much.

The major just smiled as we started shining our flashlights around the room. We were uncertain what we were searching for, but we needed to get an idea of what kind of space we were dealing with.

The internal walls were all stone. At one end of the small building there were some wooden crates that were stenciled in Arabic. I didn't know what they said. At the other end was a small semicircular niche carved in the stone wall with some additional crude stonework around it.

"That will be the Mihrab," said Major Jacobs as he shone his light over the structure. "It will be indicating the direction of the Kaaba in Mecca, the direction Muslims face when praying."

"This place doesn't look like it has been used for prayer in a very long time," said Greatrex.

There were some simply carved wooden pillars that were holding up a basic tin roof that was once painted white. Most of the noise we were still hearing came from the sand outside bouncing off the tin.

We began moving around the room, looking at possible hiding places for Winter's samples. We shook things, opened things, moved things, looked under things, as per our one-word instruction, but we found nothing. Twenty minutes later we thought we had explored all possibilities and were again gathered in the center of the building.

"Ideas, gentlemen?" I asked.

None came leaping into anyone's mind.

We kept shining our flashlights around the room, looking for something, anything that would give us a clue. I was starting to feel like a failed Indiana Jones. Then I saw it. In one corner, slightly jutting out behind some of the boxes, was a small stone plinth. It was only a few inches higher than the rest of the floor and was partially covered by the boxes we had moved in our search, so we hadn't seen it at first.

I moved over to the plinth, and the others followed. I reached my hands around the base and tried to move it. Nothing.

"Those stones look as old as the rest of the building, but the mortar work seems more recent," observed Greatrex.

Jacobs and I nodded.

"Can you pass me your screwdriver, major?" I asked.

I ran the screwdriver around the base of the plinth, trying to remove some of the mortar around it. When I had finished, I handed the tool back to Jacobs. I then crouched down with an arm around either side of the plinth and tried to move it again. Still nothing.

I put out my hand for the screwdriver again and proceeded to repeat my work on the mortar around the base. This time I dug more deeply into it, trying to remove as much as possible. It took a little time; anticipation was high, and no one spoke. When I was done, I reached down again. With every bit of strength I had left in me, I tried moving the stone. Again nothing … but then suddenly there was a small movement.

"Jack, give me a hand."

Greatrex was a strong man. He reached down with me and pushed hard as I pulled, and then we had it. The stone moved to reveal a small compartment. In that compartment was a thin metal container. It was almost like a folder but constructed of metal instead of paper. I reached in and lifted it out carefully, very carefully.

The container was sealed, and I had no intention of opening it. The three of us looked at it and then looked at each other. It had to be Giles Winter's package. It seemed we now possessed samples of some of the deadliest chemical weapons and nerve agents ever produced.

I didn't feel victorious. I felt sick.

# Chapter 24

I think it hit me right then, as I held that container in my hands. I was holding something so powerful and so evil that I had no right to be its custodian. If this material was reverse engineered, as Giles Winter had promised, it could do untold damage to thousands, or tens of thousands, of innocent people. How did I, or Jack Greatrex—anyone, for that matter—have the right to make decisions about those lives, about this material that was in my hands right now? I don't think the reality of the situation had really come home until we found and held that package.

For a few moments the only sound was the storm tearing away at the world outside.

Then the thought that I had been trying to avoid for weeks came to me like a shroud of darkness. In my hands I was holding Leyla and Amira's death sentence.

"We can't do it," I said. My voice was shaking, and I could feel my hands trembling. "We can't give this to Winter."

Another moment's silence.

"You're right." It was Greatrex. He was looking down, avoiding my eyes. As ever, he could read my thoughts. "Too many people would suffer, too many lives."

At that moment I realized what hatred really felt like. It was

Giles Winter who had put us in this position, making us choose between two terrible options, assuming we would choose to save our friends. Only a psychopath devoid of morality would put us in that position. Right then, in that moment, I loathed Giles Winter to the depth of my soul.

"No matter what the outcome of this, I will find him and I will kill him." The words felt brutal and cold as I was saying them. Then I felt myself tearing up. I looked over to my best friend. The same. I knew he would be beside me every step of the way.

"What are you saying?" The hard emotion of the moment was broken by Major Jacobs' question.

"You will need to take us to the camp's commanding officer," I said. "We'll hand this package to the authorities through him."

I thought there was a moment of confusion on Jacobs' face. "But what about your friends?" he asked.

It was then that the tears flowed, freely, embarrassingly, and despairingly.

Eventually, we replaced the plinth, secured the container under my robe, and prepared to face the sandstorm once more. Again, the storm hit us with no mercy as we opened the door and stepped into the maelstrom. Greatrex was in front; he was confident he could find our way back. I was in the middle and Major Jacobs was bringing up the rear. I kept my eyes peeled for shadowy figures in the darkness, but there were none.

Again, it was hard going, to say the least. Our breathing was labored, but we seemed to have the wind behind us for most of the journey. This gave the exposed skin of our faces some relief. We could even communicate slightly, the major correcting

Greatrex with a "right" or "left" if the big man hesitated.

Soon we were crawling through the fence between the coalition and Iraqi sectors. Jacobs motioned for us to go ahead while he performed some makeshift camouflage to try to cover our tracks. Ten minutes later he had caught up and we were pounding our way across the exposed parade ground.

Just as we left the exposed area and began to make our way down a laneway between buildings, with the wind and sand still tearing through us, I heard the major's voice.

"Gentleman, please." The words were yelled through the cacophony of the storm. "Stop here and turn right."

Greatrex, in the lead, seemed uncertain. I was sure we had been retracing our steps exactly the way we had come.

"Now if you please." The major's voice was sounding coldly insistent.

I turned around and realized why. In Jacob's hand was his service revolver, and it was making an arc, taking turns between pointing at Greatrex and me. We had misjudged this man, in a big way. It was clear this was now going to cost us dearly. Goodbye, belief in humanity.

"Continue down this laneway to the left," he pointed with his gun. We could barely hear him over the storm, but his intentions were clear. Jacobs was also standing too far behind me for me to try any clever maneuver. Besides, I had the samples of chemical weapons and nerve agents on me. No maneuver could be clever.

I didn't try to talk to him; it would be pointless in this din. I looked at Greatrex, and his eyes looked as crestfallen as my heart felt. We had trusted this man, with everything. As we walked, I went over the last twenty-four hours in my head—the crash site, the robes, the bolt cutters, the willingness to join

159

us. Everything was too damn easy; it had all fallen into place without us questioning a thing. Nicholas Sharp, sucker.

Five minutes later Jacobs commanded, "Stop here." Again, he motioned with his gun toward the door of a hut on our left. "In there."

We entered the hut through a wooden door, Greatrex first, then me. Jacobs loitered far enough behind that I couldn't kick out, but not so far that I could slam the door on his gun hand. He was clearly a professional. The room we entered was dimly lit but bright enough to see that it was empty. A few feet ahead was another door.

"Through there, please." Jacobs was used to his orders being obeyed.

In the same order we moved through the door into the next room. I could see the wheels spinning behind Greatrex's eyes. Like me, he was trying to see a way out of this. Like me, he was having no success.

The room was almost dark when we walked in—just the filtered light from a small lamp. Behind us Jacobs must have flicked a light switch; the room became almost blindingly bright. It took me a minute to adjust to the light. I could almost say *see* the light, because in that moment I surely started believing in humanity again.

Standing before me was I figure I knew all too well, a man I had not seen for a long, long time, a man who had held my life in his hands so often. He was also the man who had saved Leyla and Amira all those years ago by supplying the papers that got them out of Iraq.

"Good evening, Nicholas, Jack," said the figure before us. "You both look absolutely dreadful."

"What the ...?" Greatrex had found some words, but

probably not appropriate ones.

He had aged since I last saw him; he was grayer around the temples but still looked as fit as a bulldog. In that uninspiring, sparsely furnished military hut in the middle of a wild Iraqi sandstorm stood my former commanding officer, Colonel Colin Devlin-Waters.

After much considered thought I responded. "Shit."

Greatrex had done better.

"Colonel." I was trying to recover.

"It's actually Lieutenant General, now retired, I should point out," responded the man in front of me.

"Now, please sit down, we have quite a bit of talking to do." He indicated some wooden army-issue chairs that were arranged in a semicircle to his right.

We sat down.

# Chapter 25

The sandstorm was still hammering the world outside. I didn't hear a thing, only the words of the man before me.

"Firstly," Devlin-Waters began, "please let me apologize for our little ruse with Major Jacobs here. We knew that out there in the storm he would not be able to persuade you to change course, so to speak, so a … military escort seemed appropriate. It was urgent that I speak to you."

I looked over to the door. Jacobs had put away his gun and was pulling up a chair.

"I am very sorry," said Jacobs. "After you told me you were planning to hand the samples over to our base commander and I saw the depth of your commitment, I realized that only one man could persuade you to change your minds. The general instructed me to bring you to him, and not take no for an answer."

General Devlin-Waters nodded in agreement.

"But how could he instruct you when we were with you the whole time?" I asked.

It was Greatrex who provided the answer. "When he stayed to mend the fence, we went ahead. Radio, I presume."

Jacobs reached into his pocket and produced a small handset.

"Why?" I began. "Why do you want us to change our minds?

And while we're at it, why the hell are you, a now apparently retired Marine general, here in Iraq at all?"

I may have sounded aggressive, but I didn't mean to. I was just thoroughly confused.

"Fair enough. One step at a time, and I'll try to make everything as clear as I can," said our former boss.

We waited expectantly for the general to tell his story.

"When we were all stationed here in Iraq several years ago, some worrying rumors came to my attention. They pertained to the possibility that Saddam Hussein had done some sort of deal to get rid of his chemical weapons before the coalition invasion. We understood that in return he was promised freedom after the war. We were also told that part of the deal was that someone would keep samples of the weapons, the nerve agents, and the formulas safe for later collection. The problem was we had no idea who had made this deal or who was going to collect them."

Our former superior officer had our complete attention. The story was sounding all too familiar.

"Suspicion fell on several people. It made us begin to contemplate the concept that this was not the isolated work of one man, but rather a cartel, if you like."

"A coalition working against our coalition," said Greatrex.

"Exactly, Jack. I hope you don't mind me calling you Jack now that we're all decommissioned."

Greatrex and I both nodded in agreement, but we knew that General Devlin-Waters would never be Colin to us; too much respect had gone under the bridge for that.

"After the issue with you, Nicholas, and that poor man Akram Salib, it was logical that some suspicion would fall on Major Giles Winter. I never liked the man."

"I think we can offer you agreement on that, sir," I added. It took me a while, but I was starting to regain my equilibrium.

"Anyway, Winter was shipped out of Iraq and out of the service. I had argued against that, because I thought he was our biggest lead into this phantom cartel. I was overruled."

"He likes to call it a network," chipped in Greatrex.

The general nodded and continued. "Over time the leads ran out and we could make no case against anyone specific. We still had our suspicions, but suspicions were not enough to prosecute anybody. In the end we accepted that to some extent, our coalition, and our political leaders, had been made to look like fools. There was nothing we could do about it. No chemical weapons found, plain and simple."

"It's our understanding that Giles Winter's network influenced the media greatly to make that case," I interrupted.

"Not surprising. May I ask how you came to know this, Nicholas?"

"He told us," I responded bluntly.

The general raised an eyebrow but continued. "As time went by, I was promoted and reassigned to other duties and locations, but I always tried to keep tabs on Winter. I wasn't happy about the way things had ended."

We all took a collective break for a minute to let these new facts sink in. The storm still raged outside, as did the storm in my head as I tried to think this through.

"It was only in the last few months that we started getting snippets of information indicating Winter was on the move again. We didn't know what he was up to, but our sources told us it related back to the original issue in Iraq."

"We? ... Us?" I questioned.

"During my service and after my retirement I built up quite a circle of … friends—colleagues, if you like. These were people who, like me, worried when recalcitrants like Giles Winter got away with sanctioning suspect activities while the authorities had their hands tied with red tape."

"Sounds a bit like a star chamber to me," said an unimpressed Greatrex. "A group of people who think they can make judgments better than everyone else, including the authorities."

"I see what you mean, Jack, but no. Perhaps I have misrepresented the situation. This is not a formal group of people; we never meet, nor do we ever sanction anything against the elected government's policies. We just help with a bit of information and facilitation from time to time, and only when we are requested to by our elected leaders."

Jack Greatrex seemed pacified, and to some extent so did I.

"You and your group are still well connected to active military personnel and information, I presume?" I asked, nodding in Jacobs' direction.

"We are. It is often essential."

Another moment of relative silence. This was all seeming a little surreal.

"So, where do Nicholas and I fit into all of this?" asked Greatrex, again forthright.

"As more information was gathered, we learned there may be a connection between Winter and the upcoming USO tour. Imagine my surprise when we found out the two of you were involved with the tour. We weren't sure if that was coincidental or planned. We did, however, think it expedient to place someone on the tour to keep an eye on things."

"Who, exactly?"

"Give me a moment more, Nicholas, and all will be revealed. I will say, however, that once you confided to Major Jacobs what had occurred over the last few weeks, the ball game changed. That's when I decided to fly in to be available to speak to you if circumstances required. As it turned out, circumstances did dictate the need for this conversation."

"I think we need an answer to the most important question, sir. Why don't you want us to hand these samples and formulas over to the authorities? You must know it is at huge expense to ourselves and others close to us that we've made that decision," I asked.

"Yes, I do, and I can't begin to express how much sympathy I feel for the two of you, and for Leyla and Amira Akram in this situation. None of you did anything to deserve this."

The general looked genuinely upset. Nothing had changed my mind that this was a good man in front of us, but I could still see no solution.

"The trouble is we don't know how wide Giles Winter's network is. We don't know who we can trust and who we can't," said the general.

"Amen to that," said Greatrex.

I thought for a moment. "What if we give the samples to you, here, now?"

"I appreciate your trust, Nicholas, I really do, but the only way we are going to be done with all this is if we catch Winter in possession of the samples. Anything else won't stick. I believe he is enough of a coward to give up information on his 'network' if we have him over a legal barrel. We just can't get near him." Devlin-Waters paused for a moment; you didn't become a general without knowing how to give a good persuasive speech.

"The two of you can get close; he is expecting you. We can get to him through you, but only while you have those samples in your possession."

"What if something goes wrong?" asked Greatrex. "The ramifications are too much to even contemplate. The lives ..."

"I know, and I agree ... to some extent. The difference is now you are not alone. You have my support, along with that of my colleagues. I think we have proven so far, through Major Jacobs, how useful that support can be. That is the game changer."

The general had completed his pitch, or so we thought.

"One more thing, sir. You didn't answer our question. Who did you have keeping an eye on us?"

"Well, I'm afraid I have made a costly error there. Costly to me, and if I'm not mistaken maybe costly to you as well, Nicholas."

"Who is your man watching us on the tour? I assume he was watching us from the beginning, which excludes Major Jacobs." Greatrex spoke for us both.

"You assume correctly and incorrectly, Jack. You're right, I did have someone watching you from the beginning of the tour. I used the only real contact I have in your new industry. Where you assume wrongly is thinking it was a man. It was not; it was in fact a woman, my stepdaughter, to be specific. I think you know her well, Nicholas. Her name is Kaitlin Reed, and she has recently gone missing."

Among the kaleidoscope of thoughts and questions that were spinning around my brain I heard the general say:

"Take a few minutes, gentlemen. Whatever decision you make, we will stand behind you." With that, he and Major Jacobs walked through the door into the next room.

Jack Greatrex and I sat looking at each other in silence.

"Holy shit," he said.

I couldn't have put it better myself.

"We have about five minutes to make the biggest decision of our lives." I said.

"And it could be the last decision of Leyla's and Amira's lives."

"Not to mention Kaitlin," I added.

We sat for a moment, listening to the storm beat down on the tin roof.

"Y'know, we have no decision to make," I said after a minute or so.

"If the general thinks the right thing to do is to hang on to the samples, then it's the right thing to do." Greatrex was a great believer in trust and doing what was right.

"Plus, it gives us a possible chance of helping the girls and Kaitlin." This was the real game changer.

"We tell him?" asked Greatrex.

"We tell him."

I called the general and Major Jacobs back into the room and told them of our decision.

"Well done," he said. "I know it's a risk, but we can do this," said the general.

I liked the "we" part.

"Now," he continued, "you need to get back to your equipment and store that package."

"Before Winter's lapdog notices how long you've taken to make it back," added Jacobs.

Greatrex and I asked the general a few more questions about Kaitlin, her involvement, and her disappearance.

"She sent me a message saying she thought she knew who Winter had inside the tour, then we didn't hear from her again," he told us.

"How were you receiving messages from her?" asked Greatrex.

"We didn't know who to trust on the US side, so we communicated through a contact from the British embassy."

There was the problem.

We got up to go. After again covering ourselves in our Iraqi garb in preparation for the wild storm outside, we turned to the man who was unexpectedly sending us on yet another mission, just like old times. Both Greatrex and I shook hands with the general.

"We'll do our best to fix this, sir," I said boldly, "and we will do our best to bring back your stepdaughter." I sounded more confident than I felt.

I was sure I saw a slight tear in a good man's eye.

Jacobs opened the door, and we stepped out into the grasp of the sandstorm.

We had snatched the devil's catch. Now it was time to outrun the hounds of hell.

# Chapter 26

Everyone on the tour was tired the next day, but Greatrex and I were exhausted. It must have shown on our faces, but our bandmates had the good grace not to mention it. They were now used to us being out of step.

After we left General Colin Devlin-Waters the night before, Jacobs, Greatrex, and I had braved the storm back to where the equipment was stored. Greatrex had a key, so we let ourselves in and inserted our deadly package inside my keyboard as instructed. We then went back to our room. Once on the journey I thought I may have again seen a shadow behind us, but we had no energy or inclination to follow it up. We felt sure Winter's contact would expose themselves soon enough. As things were, it was vital to our plan that Winter was told by his man that we had possession of the weapon samples and had followed his instructions.

The rest of the tour was moving on today. They were catching a C-130 Hercules from the Taji Base at midday. They were flying directly to the Bagram Airfield, Afghanistan, where they would be joined by another band who were replacing us. We said our goodbyes midmorning and wished them all the best. They were a good bunch of people. We had shared a lot in a short space of time. Oddly, both the music industry and war did that to you—brothers and sisters in arms.

Our gear had been separated from the rest. Greatrex had supervised this, knowing the importance of one particular keyboard not going missing in action.

Our band and crew were due to fly out midafternoon. We were joining a British C-17 directly out of Taji, which was taking us to the RAF Brize Norton Airbase in Gloucestershire, England. From there it would be a reasonably short journey to the Isle of Wight for our next performance. We were all looking forward to being out of Iraq and back in civilian territory.

It was about 2 p.m. when Major Jacobs tracked us down at our quarters.

"I just wanted to say goodbye and wish you the best of luck," he said, shaking our hands. "You have a big job ahead, but you two are very determined and resourceful men."

Easy for him to say; on the other hand, I liked the major much more when he wasn't pointing a gun at us.

"By the way," he continued, "we are out of River Valley now—no more blackout—so if you want to answer that earlier message from LA, I can make our communications center available to you before you leave."

It seemed like a good idea. Among the events of the night before I had almost forgotten about the message from Kenny Medina. The major led the way.

The Skype image of Kenny Medina appeared on the screen before us. He looked tired and a little grumpy. Not surprising, as it was 4.30 a.m. in Los Angeles.

"You know I need my beauty sleep," Kenny joked. He'd probably only just gone to bed anyway; like most music people, he was a night owl.

"I've only just been able to get back to you, Kenny. We've been in blackout. Sorry about the timing, but your message said you might have some important information for us," I said, trying to soften him up.

"I'm glad to see you both alive and well, but unless it's just bad reception, you both look like crap," was his honest response.

"You're not the first to say that in the last couple of days," responded Greatrex, who was looking at the screen over my shoulder.

Kenny carried on undistracted. "I continued making a few inquiries after you left. I have a few friends who have worked on USO tours and even a couple who have worked directly for the organization."

"Go on," I said.

"Well, it took a while for my contacts to get back to me, but there was one bit of information I thought may be relevant to your situation."

We both looked at Kenny's image expectantly.

"It turns out there was an unfortunate accident. A very experienced and respected USO tour organizer turned up dead in Long Beach. The police are calling it in as an accident—drowning, in fact."

I was starting to feel a chill in that hot room.

"Do you have a name?" asked Greatrex.

"Yes, that's what confused me. I thought it was the name of the USO person working on your tour, but I may be wrong."

I felt cold.

"What was his name, Kenny?" I pleaded.

"It was Elliot Brooks."

I felt colder. I turned to Greatrex.

"How could this be?" I asked. "How could anyone get

away with impersonating a well-connected operator like that. People over here would've known he wasn't the real Elliot Brooks."

"Well, here's the thing," interrupted Kenny. "Elliot Brooks was a very experienced USO operator, but he had done all his work in the Asia Pacific region. This was meant to be his first tour of the Middle East. There was a good chance no one there would have known him."

"Damn. Hell and damn." I responded, lost for better words.

Major Jacobs was quicker to react than the rest of us. He was on the radio attempting to contact the C-130 taking our former tour mates, including the man we knew as Elliot Brooks, to Bagram. At one point we heard him say, "Are you sure? Please confirm." His voice sounded urgent.

It took a few minutes—in fact, almost twenty—before he turned to us with a pained expression on his face.

"I just heard back from the flight crew of the C-130 taking the tour to Afghanistan. They performed a thorough check of personnel on the aircraft. Elliot Brooks was not on board; he never got on the plane."

Greatrex and I looked at each other. Given the information we had received over the last few minutes, it wasn't surprising that Brooks had vanished. He had no more need of the tour nor the people on it. He did, however, need to keep an eye on us. I presumed he had also been the one "keeping an eye on us" the night before, the shadowy figure in the sandstorm.

Of one thing we were certain: we would be seeing the man who claimed to be Elliot Brooks again. Deep in my core, I hoped that meeting would not go well for him.

# Chapter 27

As we descended toward the runway at the RAF Brize Norton base in Gloucestershire, the contrast between the dry plains and deserts of Iraq and the rich color of the South-West English countryside couldn't be greater. Below us, the patchwork of green fields, hedgerows, and county lanes was a welcome sight. Our C-17 Globemaster 111 landed smoothly, and the British troops who were on the plane with us let out a cheer as we touched down on their home soil.

Just before the aircraft stopped, Robbie West announced to our group, "I've got a little surprise for you folks."

As the door opened, we saw a row of luxurious-looking chauffeured black SUVs.

"For us?" I asked.

"Absolutely. I know we would normally take a helicopter to the Isle of Wight from here, but I figured we've all had enough of chopper rides for a while, so I asked my manager to book these. We'll ride in comfort, and by the way, each vehicle has a fully stocked bar."

Now I was cheering ... on the inside.

We climbed aboard one of our black four-wheeled saviors. Greatrex and I had a vehicle to ourselves. We were barely out the front gate of the base before we were both kicking back with a scotch and surveying the passing scenery.

"Great to be a civilian again ... again," he said.

"Cheers to that," I said, raising my drink.

It was just under two hours to Southampton, where we were to catch a ferry to the island. We didn't talk much as we traveled down the A34 in our convoy. The alcohol softened our mood, but we were still deeply worried. As usual, a variety of scenarios, most of them bleak, were playing around in our heads as the green fields and small towns with enchanting names rolled by. After a while we passed through a small village ominously named World's End.

"I hope not," said Greatrex looking at the sign.

"Well, it's up to us to make sure it's not. Not for Leyla and Amira, not for Kaitlin Reed, if she's still alive, not for us, and not for anyone else." I was starting to feel a bit of grit setting in, obstinate conviction. About time.

"We need a plan of attack or at least something to build on," said Greatrex.

I responded, "It's time we were on the front foot. Every time we've stepped forward on this, Winter has pushed back. We need to commit."

Greatrex nodded.

"I'm tired of that man calling all the shots," I continued. "I do feel better that we have some sort of backup from the general out there—"

"But?" interrupted Greatrex.

"I know we have his direct line, and he can arrange people to support us if we need it, but ... it's still going to be up to us to fix this. We need to make a statement, get under Winter's skin," I said.

"So?" asked the big fella.

"If we provoke the bastard, put him under pressure, he's more likely to make a mistake, and more likely to create an opportunity for us.

"I agree, but do you have any idea how to do that?" asked the big fella.

"I do," I said. Then I explained.

Fifteen minutes later, Jack Greatrex was sitting next to me with a grin on his face.

"You know this could go bad very easily," he said.

"I know."

"But you want to do it anyway?"

"I do," I said.

Still the grin. "You know the front foot is definitely my favorite foot," he said.

Before long, the A34 and the English countryside disappeared into the outskirts of Southampton. Southampton had been a major sea port for many centuries. It has featured strongly in Britain's maritime history. The Pilgrim Fathers had sailed from there on the Mayflower in 1620. Just under three hundred years later the Titanic had sailed from the same port. Two famous journeys, two very different outcomes. I could feel the history of the ancient streets, buildings, and the waters themselves as we drove to the dock where we would meet our waiting car ferry.

The journey across the Solent took us around an hour. We arrived in East Cowes, on the Isle of Wight, in a positive state of mind. The consistent intake of scotch may have had something to do with that, but more to the point, we now had a plan.

Before we went back down to our SUVs on the ferry, Robbie gathered us together again.

"I have one more surprise for you," he announced. "As you

know, we have two days until the festival begins. I have booked
out a hotel overlooking the ocean on the southeast side of the
island. My instructions to you are to relax for a couple of days,
and when you're done with that, kick back and chill. Time for
a bit of R & R, all expenses paid." Robbie was a wealthy rock
star as well as a nice guy.

The news went down well with the band.

I smiled. So did Greatrex, but we both knew rest and
recuperation was not on our to-do list. We were just about
to enact a plan that would provoke the most dangerous man
either of us had ever met. There would be no rest, and what
we were about to do would be the opposite of recuperation. It
was a walk to the edge of a deadly abyss. We needed to build
our resolve and anticipate a world of possible bad outcomes.
Everything was at stake here. We were about to poke the bear,
and Giles Winter was going to become very unhappy with us.
There was no doubt, none … there would be consequences.
We just needed to be ready for them.

It was therapeutic to drive over the rolling island hills,
past endless majestic, historical properties, and take in the
breathtaking ocean views that the Isle of Wight offered. As
I looked out the SUV window, I was aware that one part of
me was greatly looking forward to performing for thousands
of people at the Isle of Wight Festival. What a spectacular
backdrop this landscape would make to a memorable musical
performance. We were due to play just after sundown on the
Saturday night, prime time. On the flip side, another part of
me was dreading the outcome if we got the darker side of our
work here wrong. Would this same awe-inspiring panorama
become a scene of violence and tragedy. Was it possible that
good people could die and evil could prevail among such epic

natural beauty?

Just as the conflicted philosopher in me was trying to resolve these issues, we turned off the road, passed through some large rustic gates and onto a long tree-lined rural driveway. A few minutes later it was obvious Robbie West was as good as his word. The final curve of the driveway revealed the most magnificent two-story county estate I had ever seen. Overlooking the endless blue ocean waters, Robbie's hotel was just as promised. Surrounded by elegant outhouses, lawns and a large swimming pool, this place would have been nirvana at any other time.

"Robbie has outdone himself," observed Greatrex, as our vehicles came to a stop in front of a set of majestic stone steps leading to a massive pair of double doors.

"Iraq suddenly seems a long way away," I responded.

Fifteen minutes later we had all been escorted to our separate rooms. After the hotel porter had delivered my luggage to my room and wished me the obligatory pleasant stay, I looked around. It wasn't really a room at all. Perhaps suite would be a better description. Palatial chambers would also have done the trick. An enormous bay window overlooked manicured lawns leading down to the sea. The furniture was all high-quality antique, and a chandelier hung in the center of the room from an overly high ceiling. The adjoining bedroom contained a bed the size of a small airport. My first thought was how different this was to our barracks accommodation in Al Taji. My second thought was perhaps I had died in that helicopter crash after all and fluked my way to heaven.

My thoughts were interrupted with a knock on the door. Without waiting, Greatrex walked right in.

"If it is all going to end here, I can't think of a better place to face the apocalypse."

"I hope you're overstating the downside of our mission here," I answered. "But yeah, if you've gotta go, this is a hell of a place to leave from."

We both sat down on the oversized couch.

"Time to work out the logistics and get to work," said my friend.

"A couple of things first," I began. "I guess we need to accept we have just committed a major international crime against humanity by smuggling samples of chemical weapons and nerve agents into Britain. If things go pear-shaped, a life sentence in one of her majesty's prisons awaits us for that little indiscretion."

"No, really, don't pull any punches," was the big fella's response. "Do think we could try and put that out of our minds for now?"

"Of course, but I thought it was worth mentioning." Nicholas Sharp, bringer of doom. "The next thing," I continued, "is the question of whether Winter is planning to take his package off our hands here or wait until we get back to the States?"

"It could go either way, but I'm leaning toward him making his move here."

"My thinking exactly, Watson." I had always been a bit of a Sherlock Holmes fan, although clearly I didn't display any of his detecting skills or we wouldn't be in this situation now. "We know that from the picture with the girls and the newspaper masthead that Winter is, or was, holding Leyla and Amira in South-West England. I think he has gone to the trouble of bringing them to England because he plans to act here, on the Isle of Wight. He needs them close in case we misbehave and require disciplining."

"Fair enough."

"What's more, I reckon he is probably aware that if something goes wrong, he'll need to move quickly. He will bring the girls onto the island." I was sure of that.

"That means Leyla and Amira could be on the island now."

"Highly likely, but equally likely we would never find them even if we looked. The island is a big place, and it will be flooding with people coming for the festival. Winter and his men aren't about to take the girls out shopping." I was stating the obvious again.

"So, we get to work with your plan to flush them out and push them to the point of error." Greatrex was on the money.

"First we need to get to know this environment. Neither of us have been to the Isle of Wight before; we need to be able to find our way around. We also need a car. If things change, they will change quickly, and we need to be ready and able to move."

"I'll arrange a car," volunteered Greatrex.

"Have you checked in with the crew members who are moving our stage gear from the air base to the festival site?" I asked.

"Yep, I just heard back from them before I came in here. All the gear is arriving on site as we speak. It will be stored in a shipping container marked 'Robbie West Band' in the backstage area, behind the main stage."

"And the keyboard?"

"I have asked them to put it in the container last, for easy access. I told them we needed to get to it to adjust some of the programmed sounds over the next couple of days." Greatrex was all over this. So far so good.

"Great, so next up we need to change the rules of the game," I said.

"You're sure you want to do this?"

"I'm sure," I responded. "It's a risk, but it's the only way to mess with Winter's head."

"How do you want to go about it?" Greatrex asked.

"If you can get me the car, I'll go over to the festival site and take care of it," I said.

"Done."

Two hours later I was on my way to the festival site, straightening out the twists and turns of an engaging island road in a rented black Mini Cooper S. Greatrex had done well. I like my cars, and the Mini suited me just fine. The Cooper S was like driving a rocket-powered brick.

At the VIP entrance to Seaclose Park, the festival site, the guard at the gate waved me through as soon as I showed him my access-all-areas pass. I parked and went to track down Dennis Scutt, our lighting guy. Dennis had arranged to get me a key to the container that held our gear.

Another twenty minutes later, torch in hand, I opened the container door. I quickly identified the familiar road case that contained my Nord keyboard and opened it. Another fifteen minutes' work with a screwdriver, and I had levered the end off the keyboard casing and reached in to pull out the package with the samples. Thank God it was still there. I put the package carefully on the floor, closed the keyboard and put it back in its case.

Before picking up the samples package, I quickly installed the small security camera Greatrex had provided me with, on the wall. My friend was a very resourceful man. I went back outside, locked the container doors and went back to the car.

With the samples safely and carefully placed under the front passenger seat, I drove off through the gate, waving at the guard as I passed. I didn't speed at all. Now was not the time to be pulled over by the island's police.

"You've got it?" asked Greatrex as he opened the door to his suite. It was just as luxurious as mine.

"I've got it," I said. "Did you come up with a place to store it that we can access quickly if needed?"

That had been Greatrex's job while I retrieved the samples.

"I found a drystone wall at the back of the main building. One stone was just loose enough to pull out and create a kind of small safe. The area is quiet and out of the way. I wouldn't want to leave the package there for long, but it'll do the job for now."

"Excellent," I responded. It was vital the samples were not in either of our rooms in case Winter's people came searching. Twenty minutes later the package was in its stone safe and Greatrex and I were back in my room. The sun was setting and the view over the water was magnificent.

"I wish I was enjoying this view under different circumstances," observed Greatrex.

He was not alone in thinking that.

"Well, stage one completed," I said. "The rules have now changed."

We both looked over the water.

When Giles Winter went looking for his cache, he would quickly work out what we had done. While he wouldn't yet panic, our move would have been unexpected. We knew he would be angry, very angry. We were now gambling everything on human nature. Angry people make mistakes. For all our sakes, we desperately needed Giles Winter to lose his grip on things just a little, just enough to let his temper into the room, just enough to make an error of judgment.

At last, we were pushing back.

# Chapter 28

The next morning Jack Greatrex and I left the rest of the band and crew by the enormous pool. They were nursing their hangovers and planning a day doing very little. They were also now beyond questioning what we were doing.

Our plans involved getting to know the geography of the island. We didn't know exactly how things were going to play out, but we figured there would be movement. We also figured it was most likely whatever the scenario was, it would happen on the island.

We drove the length and breadth of the Isle of Wight. From the southeast coast, where we were staying, over to St Helens and Ryde. We then doubled back the width of the island through the bustling town of Newport over to the west coast. Less populated than the east, and more rugged, the west coast of the island featured wild untamed areas where long high-speed roads and clifftop views abounded. The Mini Cooper loved the roads. After examining the extreme west of Alum Bay and Yarmouth, we headed back to Cowes. We drove past the entrance to Osborne House, the summer home of Queen Victoria and Prince Albert.

While we grabbed some lunch in East Cowes, one of the locals told us Queen Victoria loved the Isle of Wight and

Osborne House so much that she chose it as her place to die. I could understand that; the whole island was miraculously stunning. That said, neither Greatrex nor I particularly wished to follow the good Queen by meeting our demise here.

As the day was ending, we drove back up the drive to our hotel. We had no answers, and we had moved no closer to a resolution, but at least we had done our groundwork.

Greatrex went straight to his room to check the feed to the camera in the storage container. Any movement inside the container would trigger it to record automatically. This was directly relayed back to Jack's computer. It was very handy to have a tech-head around.

"Nothing," said Greatrex as he entered the majestic dining room where the band were gathered for what promised to be a memorable meal.

It was an evening of stories, laughter, and more stories. Musicians are good at telling tales. It's a life that puts people in all sorts of strange situations. It's also a life where you interact with an incredible variety of people, such as those around that table. I enjoyed the company.

Greatrex went up to his room a couple of times to check the feed to his computer, but there was no change.

We retired to the formal living room, which took the term "grand" to another level. We sat, drank, and talked, in sublime luxury.

Despite all the frivolity, the darkness wouldn't leave. In a quieter moment I asked Greatrex, "If you were Giles Winter, where on this island would you choose to make your base?"

"I think I'd go with a less populated area, my bet would be somewhere in the west," he said.

"I agree. I think the relative isolation would appeal to him,"

I responded.

It was still no real help to us. We just had to wait. I hated waiting. As it turned out, we didn't have to wait for long.

It was around 2 a.m. and I was in a restless sleep when I was awakened by an unexpected sound. For a second I was startled, but then I realized it was someone banging on my door. Trying to walk into as much furniture as I could in my half-asleep state, I went to the door and opened it. A smarter, more awake man would have asked, "Who's there?" I was not that man. Thankfully, it was Greatrex.

"Come, look," he said. "We have a mouse in our trap."

Mouse in our trap—really? I followed Miss Marple to his room.

"Look at this," Greatrex said, pointing to the screen on his laptop.

I could see nothing but a black screen. After a couple of seconds, the container lit up. Judging from the moving shadows, the light seemed to come from a powerful flashlight. As my eyes grew accustomed to the relative darkness on the screen, I began to make out the shape of a figure. The flashlight had been laid down, presumably so the figure could work with both hands. That helped us.

"Have you watched this through to the end?" I asked. "Do we know who it is?"

"No. As soon as it triggered, I went to get you."

We looked on. We could make out the figure a little better now; it looked like a male. He followed the same process I had the day before. He opened the keyboard case, got the keyboard out, and began to work on the end of the casing with a screwdriver. We still hadn't got a look at his face.

"This has all happened in the last few minutes?" I was

looking at the time stamp on the screen. "How long do you think it would take us to get to the festival site?"

"Too long."

I knew Greatrex was right, so we kept looking at the screen.

Our man reached into the keyboard. It was the first time he appeared to hesitate. The figure pulled his hand out and then reached in again. He found nothing. Of course, we already knew that would be the case. With his body language looking slightly more agitated, the figure turned the keyboard around and unscrewed the other end. His hand went in and came back out again. Still nothing. His body language was growing extremely unsettled and intense. It was then that he turned to look around the container—what had he missed?

Our shadowy intruder then turned all the way around. The torch on the ground now lit his whole face. It was an angry face, it was a frustrated face, and it was a confused face. Jack and I glanced at each other. It was the face of the man we knew as Elliot Brooks.

It was 3 a.m. Greatrex and I had been talking for almost an hour.

"Well, there you go. It will definitely all go down on the Isle of Wight," said my friend.

"And that lowlife Brooks," I responded, "or whatever the hell his name is, has put himself right in the center of this, and you know what, I'm glad we'll get our hands on him."

There was no doubt in either of our minds that Elliot Brooks was directly behind the abduction and possible murder of Kaitlin Reed. He was obviously also a very trusted member of Giles Winter's entourage.

"I think we shall be hearing from Mr. Winter shortly," said Greatrex. "I suspect that sometime tonight, if not already, he's going to receive news that will make him a very unhappy man."

"The question now, the life-altering question, is who will he direct his frustrations at?" I added.

We couldn't go back now; we had committed. We were now banking everything on our suspicion that Giles Winter would come after us rather than risk losing or hurting his human trump cards, Leyla and Amira.

A few minutes later I was back in bed, but my mind wouldn't shut down. I didn't know how much more sleep I would get. There was something niggling at me, not for the first time in the last few weeks. We couldn't change our strategy now; it was too late for that. The situation could turn bad in an instant. I knew the greatest likelihood was that I was going to personally confront Giles Winter. I wanted to. No one was making me. It was my own moral compass pointing me in that direction. What worried me the most was how I felt about that. Just as I had on the hill overlooking the house in the Rogue Valley, I began to feel the stirrings of anticipation and excitement within me. Damn!

I must have dozed off because again I awoke to the sound of loud knocking on my door. I clambered out of bed, forcing myself to wake up.

As I reached for the doorknob I managed to say, "Greatrex, what do you want this—" before I was abruptly cut off by the acute pain of someone's fist smashing into my face. I fell backward onto the floor, only to feel a compressing pain on my chest. It was a foot.

"Not a word, Mr. Sharp."

I recognized the voice, but I couldn't place it. My senses were reeling from the punch and I was trying to get a grip. As my eyes focused, I looked up to see the sadistic face of Santori,

Giles Winter's number one man.

"Make no sound; you don't want innocent lives needlessly lost here because you called for help." Santori, the humanitarian.

I heard scuffling behind him. Santori removed his foot from my chest and stepped to one side. In the doorway was Rowley, Santori's playmate from the Mojave Desert. Also present was Winter's third man. I recognized him from Leyla's house in Portland. Between them stood a struggling Jack Greatrex, his arms held behind him by the two enforcers. Greatrex did not look happy.

Once Greatrex was bundled inside and the door behind him closed, I was allowed to get up. I held my jaw; it hurt like all hell. We were marched to the couch and told to sit.

The door to my room opened again and in walked the second most hated man in my universe, the fake Elliot Brooks. He displayed his usual smug smile and condescending manner. I did, however, briefly detect a little urgency or fear of some sort on his face.

"Nicholas Sharp, how nice to see you again ... in no way whatsoever." He was so welcoming.

"Brooks, or whatever the hell your name is," was all I could spit out.

Greatrex tried to get up off the couch. I presumed he intended to beat Brooks to a pulp, but he was stopped by Rowley's fist.

"Yes, call me Brooks for now," said Fake Brooks. "I don't want to confuse you with real names. You two must have realized that you've made a mistake, a stupidly big mistake."

To look at him and hear him was to want to hit him.

"Mr. Winter is a generous and forgiving man." Brooks could

not lie straight in bed.

"In the tradition of Hitler," I said. That cost me a slap on the face from Santori, but it was worth it.

"As I was saying," continued Brooks, "Mr. Winter is willing to forgo hurting anyone close to you if you tell us right now where the samples and formulas are."

"And if we don't?" It was Greatrex asking.

"And if you don't, you will face a consequence that you will deeply regret for the rest of your lives." The he added, "However long that is."

"You're full of crap, Brooks," I said. "If you hurt the girls, you lose your hold on us and risk losing those samples forever." I felt good about saying that.

Silence. Uncomfortable silence.

"Well?" Brookes asked.

I always liked it in movies when the hero said, "Go to hell," so I said, "Go to hell." That felt good as well, for at least five seconds until Santori's fist connected with my face. I shouldn't watch so many movies.

Though I was feeling full of bravado, I was also relieved that they had come after us, not the girls. I was also scared of what would happen if we got this wrong.

"You are fools," announced Brooks. He turned to the other three. "Search both their rooms. I'll watch them." Then he pulled out a gun and pointed it in our direction.

For around forty minutes we sat there saying nothing. There was more hatred than air in that room. The hatred was from both sides.

When Brooks' offsiders reported back, they had nothing, and Brooks was clearly annoyed. That made me happy.

"For the last time, where are the samples?"

Silence.

"Very well. What happens next has been determined by your foolish decisions." Brooks' patronizing smile reappeared. "You are correct in saying that Mr. Winter has no intention of harming the girls at this point in time. I stress the condition 'at this point in time.' There will, however, be a substantial consequence for the path you have chosen."

Brooks paused, as though waiting either for applause or a reaction. He got nothing from us.

"Shortly, we will talk again. At that point you will voluntarily bring the samples to us." Speech finished.

Brooks nodded to his men and they all turned and left.

For a couple of minutes Greatrex and I sat in silence. We were both a little worse for wear but would be all right. A slight smirk had crept onto my friend's face.

"Did you notice that each time he mentioned his hostages, he said 'the girls'? He didn't mention Leyla or Amira by name."

"I noticed," I said.

"Does that mean there's a chance Kaitlin is alive and they're holding her here as well?" he asked.

"It's possible," I continued, "but what worries me the most is what the hell are they planning? Brooks clearly said that in the short term they're not going after the girls, and they don't appear to be coming after us."

"But they are coming after someone, and probably someone close to us, but who?" asked Greatrex.

"I have no idea," I said. I was deeply worried. What innocent party had we accidently dragged into this mess? I couldn't help but feel that in our need to force Giles Winter's hand, we may have underestimated his response. If he had his way, there was going to be a price to pay. The question was, who was going to pay it?

# Chapter 29

Late that afternoon our convoy of black SUVs headed to the festival site, just out of the township of Newport. I was feeling exhausted and more than a little anxious. Greatrex had gone ahead some hours before in our rented Mini Cooper. As usual, it was his job to make sure my equipment was set up.

We had talked through the morning about ways this could play out. We needed to be as prepared as we could for any move Winter, Brooks, or their men may make. This was important not only for our safety but also for those around us. For this reason, we decided to break with Greatrex's usual duties while the band was on stage. Normally, he would be side of stage, out of sight of the audience, ready to act if anything went wrong with the gear. He would also pass me my guitar when needed. For this show we had decided that once we started playing, Jack should be out in the audience, ready to react to any situation if required. We didn't think Winter would try anything in such a public environment, but we were taking no chances.

To help with communication, Greatrex had procured a simple two-way radio system. It included earbuds, to be unnoticed, and hidden lapel microphones for the same reason. He and I could remain in contact while the band was on stage.

As we pulled through the gates into the festival grounds, I prayed that no harm would come to any of our innocent musician friends. They had done nothing to deserve being part of this.

The atmosphere at a big music festival is exciting enough for an audience. For a band performing, it is simply electrifying. Over fifty thousand people coming to lose themselves in music and party like there's no tomorrow. The festival had several stages, but all the big names would perform on the main stage. It was a huge scaffolded structure with a roof, a giant screen either side, and hundreds of lights pointing downward across the stage area. Spiraling out of the audience were two large lighting towers. These were at least fifty feet high and held a huge array of lights, including follow spots, which could follow any performer across the stage and scan over the crowd. Between the towers was a smaller scaffolded structure; it held the sound desk and the main lighting console. The show would be produced and controlled from there.

I could see all this from where I stood. Once we had dropped off our personal gear to a very luxurious VIP tent set behind the main stage, I had climbed the stairs to the side-of-stage area. The view was fantastic. The whole thing about a music festival was to keep the music as constant as possible; keep the people entertained and minimize the downtime.

I was watching a young but well-known English band. I had heard their first two albums and liked them, but live on stage these guys were over the top. The rhythm section was hot, and the singer owned the room. The three-quarter-capacity crowd were responding with energy and enthusiasm. It was late afternoon, so you could still see clearly across the ocean of enthralled faces. The stage lights were all on and enhancing the mood, but they wouldn't come into full effect until the sun went down. We were due to play about an hour after sundown. Scheduled to play after us was another legendary band, part of Britain's rock royalty.

After twenty minutes of enjoying the music and the atmosphere, I returned to our tent. I checked in with Greatrex to make sure all was fine with my set-up. We then excused ourselves and went outside to a more private area.

Greatrex produced a set of earbuds and a lapel mic from his pocket. "Put these on and we'll check them now," he said.

I put them on. They were perfectly concealed, so well so that I didn't even realize Greatrex was already wearing his. No one in the band or audience would notice them.

"The transmitter for these just looks like part of the keyboard rig at the side of the stage," said my friend. "Now go for a walk—say, three hundred feet away, toward the catering tent—and we'll test them."

I did as instructed.

Three hundred feet away I could hear Jack Greatrex's voice as though we were in the same room.

"Are you picking me up?" I asked through my lapel mic.

"Sure," was his response.

We were in business. I just hoped that if we needed them, the microphone and transmitter would work just as well over the noise of the band and the crowd. The truth was, I hoped we wouldn't need them at all.

"Fifteen minutes, folks." It was the voice of the festival stage manager letting us know how long until stage time. Musicians prepare for big shows—any shows, really—in different ways. There are those who sit in a corner quietly, those who warm up their voices very loudly. Some talk a lot as the nervous energy starts to take hold. It's increasingly rare for professional musicians to overmedicate with alcohol or other drugs. It is a very competitive game, and if you are off yours, eventually you won't be asked back. That said, there are still countless stories that are part of rock 'n' roll folklore of musicians being poured onto the stage in a heavily "affected" state. That wouldn't be the case today. I had downed my prerequisite scotch to loosen up a little, but no more, especially on a night like this. I was sitting quietly in a corner, not being anti-social but not being social either. Robbie caught my eye and wandered over.

"Everything all right, Nicholas?" he asked.

"Sure, Robbie, just going through the process," I responded.

From the look on his face I don't know if Robbie bought my explanation, but he didn't push any harder. I was in fact "processing the show" in my head. I was also picturing every possible bad thing that I thought could happen over the next ninety minutes or so.

There was a mighty roar from the crowd as we walked on stage. Barry Flannigan and I acknowledged the roar with raised arms but neither of us looked up. There would be time for that in a couple of minutes. A moment later, Brian Pitt was surveying the scene from the drum kit like a king on his throne. He made eye contact with each of us to be sure we were ready. The adrenaline had kicked in; we were focused and ready to rumble. Brian held his drumsticks in the air and slammed them together as he counted one, two, three, four ... we were away.

If the crowd could roar at us, we could explode back at them. The thunder that was the drums hammering across the audience was like Thor himself had visited upon us. As guitar and bass joined in, a mania of driving rhythm was sent into

196

the night like attack dogs looking for prey. On cue I joined in with a powerful synthesizer and Hammond organ wash. The wall of sound was complete.

One minute into playing, we all backed off a little and a deep voice sounded over the monstrous PA system. "Ladies and gentlemen, Mr. Robbie West …"

The audience seemed to morph into a giant breathing beast as they went crazy. Robbie ran onto the stage and acknowledged his fans with two arms raised to the night sky. He grabbed his microphone off the stand and wailed like an angry angel.

It was then that I looked up and soaked in the intoxicating environment before me. It was totally dark now, so the lights were weaving a magical array of colors across the stage. We could hear and feel the audience but could only see the first few rows. This didn't stop the crowd from energizing us on to play harder and better. We were giving it everything. Every now and again the audience appeared out of the night as either a roving follow spot lit some of them up, or the blinders, the bright white lights that framed the stage but pointed out to the crowd, flashed on. Now you see them, now you don't.

As the energy continued to build, we excited, caressed, and saddened the audience as we went from hard rock and dance tracks to ballads and pop. The deal was simple. We will give our all if you give your all, and they did. Robbie was his usual charismatic self. Our front man could entice a small crowd into friendship for life. With a crowd this size, Robbie seemed to kick it up another notch. He was preaching to fifty thousand disciples.

As we settled in to our groove and each song went by without incident, I started to feel a little more relaxed. Jack Greatrex had disappeared from the side of the stage and was out in the crowd. He was looking and searching, although we didn't know for what. We had tried out our new transmitter system again. We could both hear each other, but when the crowd was in full voice, it was difficult. From my position I surveyed the crowd from the stage as much as possible, but my view depended entirely on lighting over which I had no control. I also had a job to do on stage, and that was taking a lot of focus and energy.

It seemed like a few minutes, but it was nearly an hour and a half after our show started that we began our second-to-last song. It was an up-tempo belter that the entire audience seemed to know. It had been another huge hit for Robbie in days gone past. I was playing guitar for this one, so I moved in front of my keyboard rig. This gave me a slightly better view of the crowd as I moved forward. We were all bathed in sweat but loving every second of it. The crowd now seemed like they were part of the band as we lifted each other higher and higher. The song was arranged so that Brian Pitt would have a drum solo about three quarters of the way through. Robbie would step out to one side of the spotlights, Brian would thunder his way into the audience's hearts, and then Robbie would step back into the spotlight to lead the cheers for Brian as he finished. We did this at every big show; it was always a crowd-winning moment.

As we began the song, I could feel the relief starting to wash over me; we were almost done and nothing untoward had happened. I almost called Greatrex back to his normal position at side of stage but then decided not to, not just yet. We were coming up to the drum solo, Robbie introduced Brian and stepped back. The thunder began, lights were flashing everywhere in time with Brian. The follow spots and blinders were sweeping over the crowd, lighting them up and whipping them into a frenzy.

I was enjoying the energy and drive of the drums and the crowd. I could feel Brian's rhythms pulsating through the stage floor. It was then that I looked up. The blinders had lit up the crowd at exactly the time the spotlight on the left-hand tower had lit up the right-hand lighting tower. For a split second night had turned into day, and my heart stopped. On top of the right tower I could clearly make out, if only for a second, the muzzle of a sniper rifle pointing toward the stage. Then the lights moved on and the tower went dark. The deadly vision was gone. I went cold. Stunned with fear, I realized exactly what was about to happen, and there was nothing I could do about it.

"Greatrex, Greatrex!" I yelled into my lapel mic. No response. This was the loudest part of the show. The crowd was going wild. He couldn't hear me, and even if he could there was nothing he could do in time to prevent this awful thing from happening. Brian was coming to the end of his solo. Through the lights I could see Robbie standing in shadow, preparing to step back into the main spotlight. Each stroke of Brian's drumsticks performing rim shots on his snare drum resounded around the arena like a gunshot ... just like a gunshot.

I had no time to think, just react, but not as a musician. I ran across the front of the stage just as Robbie took his first step into the light. I connected with him on his second step as he was raising his hands to lead the applause. I pushed hard, sending the singer off-balance and reeling backward toward a row of amplifiers. He looked confused—he was confused. At the precise moment I pushed him, I heard one rim shot sound slightly different from the rest. I looked down. A section of the wooden stage at my feet splintered into small pieces. It was exactly where Robbie would have been standing. Robbie saw it too. He was getting to his feet but was now pale and silent.

No one else on stage had noticed anything except for the fact that Nicholas Sharp was acting like a crazed idiot. Certainly, no one in the crowd had heard the bullet or seen the eruption of splinters. They all thought this was all part of the show, with one exception.

"Nicholas, Nick, can you hear me?" It was Greatrex.

"Left-hand lighting tower, sniper rifle, we're all good here. Go get him," was my terse response.

I looked out to the tower. I knew Greatrex would be heading that way fast. I could just make out the shape of a person climbing down the tower. He had a case strapped to him. From the stage it looked like a soft electric guitar case, also just big enough to hold a rifle.

"He's coming down the tower, he'll be gone in two minutes," I yelled.

"I'm on it," responded Greatrex. He sounded out of breath.

I looked around. With Robbie not stepping up to carry on with the rest of the song, Brian had continued to provide a soundtrack to our drama with his explosive solo. While he didn't know what was going on, he wouldn't stop the show for anything. I ran over to Robbie.

"You all right?" I asked.

"Never been better." He was a trooper. "Is it safe now?"

"Safe as houses. Greatrex is on it."

From his state of confusion, it only took a couple of seconds for Robbie, the consummate professional, to come to terms with the situation.

"The last thing we need is fifty thousand people stampeding out of here. People would get hurt, or worse," he said.

It was at that moment, Robbie West, a man who I already liked and admired, earned my lifelong admiration.

"Thanks, Nick. Now let's finish this damn show."

I reached out my hand. He took it, jumped up, and stepped straight back into the spotlight, virtually standing on the splintered hole in the stage.

"Ladies and gentlemen, Mr. Brian Pitt on the drums ..."

The crowd roared.

# Chapter 30

I didn't know what to do next. There was no point in me running out into the audience. Greatrex and our fugitive sniper would be too far ahead for me to get close, even if I could find them in the throng.

"Jack, can you hear me?" I shouted into the mic.

Nothing.

We finished the song, and I put my guitar aside. It was time for me to start the final number with my usual piano introduction. There was nothing else I could do, so I started playing. At least this song began quietly, so I might hear Greatrex. The song began.

"Nicholas, can you hear me?" It was Greatrex.

"Loud and almost clear," I responded.

"He got down the tower and into the crowd before I got there, but I'm following."

"Okay."

I looked into the crowd, I thought a few people at the front were looking at me curiously. The piano player who seems to talk to himself as he plays.

"Anything I can do?" I asked into the mic.

"I'll get back to you in a minute."

We continued playing, my fingers working from muscle

memory. My mind was with Greatrex as he pursued Robbie West's would-be assassin through the crowd.

"Nick?"

"I'm here."

"He's heading toward the VIP car park. You could probably cut him off if you go now," instructed my friend. He was breathing hard.

As the last chord of the song sounded, I was off the stage and down the stairs. I was aware people were looking at me, but I didn't care.

"How will I recognize him? I didn't get a decent look from the stage." I yelled into my mic as I ran.

"You didn't need to," responded Greatrex. "He's still got the case, plus he turned around to see if he was being followed just as the lights lit him up. I saw him."

"And?"

"Nick, it was Elliot Brooks."

"Shit. But no surprise, I suppose." I was running between rows of tents. More curious looks—care factor: zero.

"I'm almost at the car park," I yelled.

"Likewise."

Greatrex and I entered the VIP car park from different ends at almost the same time. I looked in the direction he was pointing and saw a dark figure with a guitar case slung over his shoulder. The figure was opening a car door. It was a dark-colored, nondescript Ford, and it was too far away. I wasn't going to make it in time, and neither was Greatrex. Elliot Brooks turned around, looked at me, his face showing his usual obnoxious smirk. Then he threw the case onto the back seat, climbed in and slammed the door. A second later the car wheels spun in the dirt as he took off up the track.

"Greatrex, get our car," I yelled.

Jack Greatrex was on it before I even got the words out. As I looked around, he was climbing into our black Mini. He started the engine and was on me in about three seconds. I jumped in.

"Go," I screamed.

He was already going. I was glad we had a vehicle that was fast in the dirt. In no time at all we seemed to be almost on Elliot Brooks' car.

I had hope.

Then I didn't.

Elliot Brooks pointed a handgun out his passenger-side window and fired three shots at us in quick succession. Two missed our car but one hit a headlight, taking it out. I thought we'd now have to be a little more circumspect in our pursuit. Greatrex didn't; he seemed to take no notice and accelerated up the road like he was starting a grand prix.

We were following Brooks as closely as we dared. The island roads were not designed for high-speed pursuits, and both cars were pushing their maximum capabilities. At first I thought we were heading back toward East Cowes, but then Brooks took a sharp left and we were headed west. He seemed to detour on and off the major roads as if trying to lose us, but we stuck to him. We had come too far in this whole despicable journey to let go now.

Before long we had bypassed Yarmouth and were heading south on a narrow road on the west coast of the island. Brooks clearly knew the island better than we did. We couldn't see much in the darkness, and although it was only in our single headlight beam for a second, I thought I saw a sign saying the road we were on was not open to the public.

We were traveling very fast now, and the Mini was scream-ing with pain around some of the tight corners. Greatrex was focused on nothing but the road and the car ahead. I looked to my right and saw the dark waters of the Solent, the moon reflecting on the white tops of the waves below. The only thing between our rapidly moving car and the water was a tiny section of grass leading to the edge of an alarmingly high cliff. Several times our rear wheels left the asphalt. Each time I thought we were done and were going to go over the edge, but Jack Greatrex was a very capable driver, and each time he brought us back onto the road. I, of course, was a terrible passenger; it was a control freak thing.

Brooks, who also knew how to drive, had pulled about fifty yards ahead of us when he rounded a corner and disappeared. We followed. Greatrex accelerated, the Mini's engine howling as we rounded the same bend. Out of nowhere we were suddenly blinded by an incredible white light. I couldn't see a thing and, more to the point, Greatrex couldn't see a thing. He pounded on the brakes in a racing-style stop. The car slid sideways and spun around.

It seemed like forever that we slid over the grass, the cliff edge beckoning us like the devil himself. I had just decided we were done for when the car stopped. We were facing the water but could see no grass between us and the clifftop. It was a matter of inches.

My next thought was why could we see at all—where had that light come from? I looked over my shoulder to see three cars with their headlights, on high beam, directed at the bend we'd just been negotiating. There appeared to be men standing between the cars. I couldn't make them out, but I could make out the familiar silhouettes of automatic machine guns

205

strapped around their shoulders.

Brooks hadn't been trying to lose us; he'd been trying to make sure we trailed him.

Like a couple of frenzied foxes, we had followed him directly into a trap.

Before either of us could climb out of the car, two dark figures appeared either side of us.

"Out." It wasn't a very polite invitation. It's never very polite when someone is pointing a gun at you.

We climbed out of the Mini, careful not to step too close to the cliff edge. The men pointed in the direction of the other cars with their gun barrels.

"Move."

We moved. As my eyes grew accustomed to the bright light, I recognized the two men behind us. One was Rowley, the other was the third of Winter's enforcers from Portland, still unnamed.

Of course, I wasn't surprised when Elliot Brooks stepped out from behind the lights. It was also no surprise when Giles Winter appeared next to him. All feelings of anything but anger disappeared when I saw him. I felt no fear, no frustration, no shame in our situation here on the clifftop. I only felt cold, hard fury.

"Mr. Sharp, Mr. Greatrex, you have disappointed me and made me very upset."

"Go screw yourself, Winter," I responded.

I waited a second, but there was no thump on the back of my head.

Winter ignored me and continued.

"First you removed the chemical weapons and nerve agent samples and have withheld them from me. Huge, huge mistake.

Then, by a stroke of amateur luck, you managed to stop Brooks here from delivering the message I had planned to send to you, via the death of your friend Robbie West."

"Next time you have something to say, just say it to our faces," said Greatrex. I could feel his hatred from where I stood.

"Yes, I plan to. In fact, I'll do it right now."

Winters raised the pistol that I hadn't seen in his hand and pointed it directly at Jack Greatrex.

Now I felt fear.

"No," I yelled.

"All right," Winter responded. He was playing with us.

I was relieved, but only for a second, as Santori then appeared from out of the darkness. He was not alone. He was dragging the struggling figure of a small child, an eight-year-old girl. It was Amira.

"Amira, sweetheart, are you okay?" I felt my voice break.

"Uncle Nick. Yeah, I'm all right, kind of."

That sweet little girl was on the verge of tears, but trying to be strong, almost making it. She was her mother's daughter.

"Don't worry, little one," I tried to assure her. "We'll get through this."

"She might get through this, Sharp. You certainly won't. As I said, you have made me extremely annoyed."

That was enough for Amira; she burst into tears.

"Shut up, child," was Winter's response.

I thought I'd been scared when Winter pointed his gun at Greatrex. But even that paled against the depth of emotion I felt right then. It was like nothing I'd ever experienced as I watched Giles Winter raise his gun and point it directly at Amira.

"You bastard," were the only words that came out.

Winter turned to look at me. It was not the look of a sane man, but it was the look of a very dangerous one.

"How do you feel right now, Nicholas Sharp?"

His gun was still pointing at Amira. She was trembling.

"Do you feel scared?" he continued. "You should. Do you feel like a failure? You should feel that too."

I said nothing. Greatrex said nothing. We had wanted to make Giles Winter angry, put him off his game. Now I just wanted to keep him calm, at least until his gun was pointing at somebody else.

"Now, let's be clear." Winter was speaking like a man possessed. "In the last few minutes I have shown you that I, and I alone, completely control the lives of you, your best friend, and this little girl of whom you are so fond. Remember this feeling, Nicholas. Remember how stupid you have been and how helpless you are right now."

I would not forget, ever. I just stared blankly at Giles Winter. I was soaked in defeat.

"Let's add to the equation the lives of the two ladies. Yes, that's right, your friend Leyla and the young lady that I believe you have taken quite a shine to, Kaitlin Reed, are both here on the island as well."

I wanted to feel relief that both Kaitlin and Leyla were alive, but hope had abandoned me.

"Now, let me tell you how this is going to work. People are going to die tonight. I think from the look on your face you have realized that already. It is now a question of numbers, collateral damage if you like. Your actions, and yours alone, will decide how many people will die and who they will be."

Winter was still pointing the gun at Amira. She was still shaking.

Nothing from me.

"I assume that the chemical samples are somewhere here on the island?"

I nodded.

"You are going to get in your car, get them, and bring them to me. You have ninety minutes to do this. In exactly ninety minutes, if you do not arrive, and arrive alone, the first death will occur. Another person close to you will be shot every ten minutes after that, until you arrive."

I heard a grunt. It was Greatrex. I could see him start to surge forward. It was a futile gesture among so many armed men, but he was blinded by outrage. He had the look of a man who just didn't care anymore.

He went for Winter, but he had no chance.

"Jack, no," I shouted.

At that moment Rowley appeared behind Greatrex and raised his gun.

"No," I screamed again.

At the last minute, Rowley spun his gun around and brought the butt forcefully down on the back of Jack Greatrex's head. My friend crumpled to the ground, unconscious.

Winter just continued to speak, as though nothing had happened.

"To illustrate my compassion, I will leave the young girl as the last to be eliminated." He pointed the gun away from Amira and back toward me.

This man gave new meaning to the term "calculated murder."

"You will meet us at the old military battery at the end of this road. Jack Greatrex will stay here with us. He will be the first to be killed. You have precisely ninety minutes to save him, Sharp. I suggest you get moving."

He then waved his gun toward our car. I began to move toward the vehicle. I was beyond numb.

"Oh, and one more thing, Sharp."

I just wished Winter would shut up, but I turned around. I had no choice.

"If there is any sign that you have enlisted help, any help at all, everyone will be shot immediately. If we hear one gunshot, one rustle in the grass, that's all it will take. Do you understand?"

I nodded. I understood.

# Chapter 31

As I drove back along the winding roads that Greatrex and I had traveled a short time earlier, I started weighing up my options. I was driving at speeds only marginally slower than we had on the way in. The driving seemed to focus my thoughts.

I had once been a well-respected Marine Scout Sniper. I was good at my job. The qualities that had made me good at my job, or at least the ones that I thought had made me good, were my ability to stay calm under immense pressure, analyze a situation quickly, and then act swiftly. In the past I had been able to keep all emotion out of the picture when required. It was the same with any professional shooter.

These were almost the complete opposite attributes needed to be a professional musician. A musician needed to call on a variety of emotions at any time, and to inhale the excitement of those around them. As I thought this through, I realized that Nicholas Sharp, conflicted man, was going to have to step aside. The former Nicholas Sharp, the calm, analytical, lethal version of me, was going to have to step up. Up to this point, emotion had been a big part of everything Greatrex and I did since Leyla and Amira first disappeared. Emotion had clouded my thinking and my judgment; in turn, it had impacted on my actions.

The more I processed this, the more I felt a cold, hard analytical resolve envelop me. To save those I loved I needed to be the man I was, not the man I am. So be it. No more talk of love. No more emotion. It was unaffordable.

I drove on into the night.

Just out of Newport I dialed the number the general had given me. He answered within two rings. I brought him up to date. He let out a sigh of relief when I told him his stepdaughter, Kaitlin, was still alive. I had two requests of him. He had people on the island ready to help, so I asked him to deliver some small arms weaponry to our hotel. He told me this had already been done, just in case we needed them. You don't get to be a general without thinking ahead of the game. My second request was for him to have a crew stand by to clean up later. I didn't know quite what or who they would be cleaning up, but I knew it was going to get messy back at the old battery on the cliff.

The general had wanted to send a small team in to help me confront Winter. I declined. One inkling that I was not alone would send Giles Winter into a murderous rage. That could not be chanced.

General Colin Devlin-Waters asked about my plan. I told him. I thought I had a ten percent chance of success at best, the general thought it was significantly less.

I didn't care. It was my plan.

I returned to the hotel. Its luxury seemed insulting and isolated amid the events of the evening. I retrieved the chemical weapon and nerve agent samples from Greatrex's hiding spot, found some guns and knives on the top shelf of the closet in my room, where the general's men had deposited them earlier, and was back in the car in ten minutes.

I fine-tuned my plan, if it really was a plan, as I drove back to the west side of the island. First I had to get through the Newport area before the festival traffic began to leave the site. I looked at my watch; it would be close.

Time and timing were the only things I had on my side. Giles Winter should have sent a man with me to retrieve the samples, but he was overconfident that I wouldn't risk anyone's life. This was his first mistake; he misread me. I wasn't going to risk anyone's life. I was going to risk everyone's life. I didn't blame him, I had misread me too.

I had ninety minutes to be back at the battery on the cliffs. Because the samples were at my hotel, I only needed sixty minutes for the return trip. I had bought thirty minutes to prepare for my meeting with Winter as I saw fit. Winter's second mistake was the location he'd chosen. He thought access would be difficult, and defending it, hiding his hostages, and keeping me confused would be easy. He was mostly right except that, although deserted at night, the old battery was a known tourist location by day, so a map or plan would be easily available online. It had taken me two minutes to locate it on my phone. Of course, at night there would be no tourists or interlopers; the battery would be inhabited only by the ghosts of soldiers past.

When I turned onto the clifftop road on the west side of the island, I slowed down and turned off my one remaining headlight. It was a very difficult and precarious drive in the darkness. Slowing down would cost me precious minutes, but that couldn't be helped. As I approached the area where Winter and his men had stopped us, I pulled the car off the road as much as possible. I was banking on Winter not having guards stationed this far along the road. I presumed he had limited personnel with him. Brooks, Rowley, Santori, Portland man and Winter himself had been present for the confrontation on the clifftop. It was therefore logical to presume he had at least one or two more men guarding Leyla and Kaitlin. I thought it unlikely he would have more men with him, as he'd have to make a swift and inconspicuous departure when this was all over. That meant with Greatrex out of action, there were probably seven of them and one of me. Better not to dwell on those odds. It would be my first job to try to even things up a little.

I left the car and went overland by foot in the direction of the battery. As I rose over the last rise, the view was breathtaking. A bright moon lit the old buildings and their surrounds. The clifftop concrete platforms that were the former gunnery positions towered over the white-capped waters below. At the end of a row of sheer chalk stacks appearing out of the water was an automated lighthouse casting an intermittent beacon across the waves.

At any other time, I'd stop and take it all in. Not now. The disadvantage of a bright moon meant it would be hard to get close to any of the buildings without being seen. The advantage of the bright moon meant that I could get a good look at the layout of the area and maybe even spot some of Winter's men.

I figured that Winter's people would probably be focused on the road, waiting for me to arrive. They would, however, have an ear and eye out for some sort of mass assault in case I had enlisted help. I banked on the fact they wouldn't expect or notice a one-man reconnaissance team coming over the hill. There was very little cover on this windswept coastline, so I had to crawl on my belly as I made my way down the hill. I was aware time was passing, and I only had a few minutes before I needed to return to my car to make my formal entrance.

In front of a steep earth embankment that rimmed the land side of the battery was a deep ditch, and on top of the embankment was a six-foot wire fence. There was a bridge over the ditch and a break in the embankment where the main entrance was. Winter's men had obviously used bolt cutters to cut the chain on the large metal gate and enter. I could make out one of Winter's men at the gate; I didn't recognize him. I would have to find another way in. I moved along the embankment, keeping as low as possible.

At the end furthest from the gate, still crawling on my stomach, I scaled the embankment and cut my way through the wire using some bolt cutters I had procured from the maintenance shed at our hotel. Without stopping to notice if I'd been seen, I slid down the far side of the embankment and sprinted across what looked like an old parade ground.

Staying as much in the shadows as possible, I made my way toward what I knew from the map to be an underground tunnel entrance. This gate had also been forced open. It would have been suicide for me to attempt to enter the tunnel; it would also guarantee instant death to any prisoners kept inside, so I didn't go in. Every fiber of my body was telling me that was the most likely place Jack, Kaitlin, Leyla, and Amira were being kept, but now was not the time.

I deposited a small package in the shadows near the entrance to the tunnel. I then moved over to the gun placements near the clifftop. There were two ancient cannons occupying two of the sections, and the other two sections were empty. I placed another package out of sight under one of the guns.

Sneaking a quick look at my watch, I realized I was running way behind time. I had to move quickly if I was to keep my appointment with Winter on schedule. Once more I sprinted across the parade ground, up the embankment, through the fence, down the ditch and up the hill as fast as I could. If I was late for the meeting with Winter, it would cost Jack Greatrex his life.

I abandoned any care about being seen as I scurried up the hill. I felt exposed, but I had no choice. I don't know how, but I wasn't spotted. As it turned out, any relief I felt about that was premature.

Just as I went over the hill, I came face to face with Winter's Portland man. He was as surprised as I was, but I was better trained. He went to reach under his jacket for his gun. Sometimes a knife is faster than a gun, I pulled mine out of the scabbard on my belt and plunged it through his heart. Nothing personal, no emotion—this was purely professional.

I checked behind me; we were over the brow of the hill, so no one would have seen us. Because I used a knife, no one would have heard anything either. As I briefly looked over the top of the hill to make sure, I noticed something I had missed before: one of Winter's cars was missing; that troubled me. I retrieved the knife and ran toward my car. The odds were now six to one.

I went over possibilities in my mind as I sprinted toward the location where I had parked the Mini. One or more of Winter's men had to be checking the road. If he found my car, this was all over. My only hope was that I was heading overland in a straight line, but the road meandered. I ran faster.

As I went over the last hill toward where my car was parked, my heart sank. Another car, one of Winter's, was parked beside mine. Its lights were shining on my empty driver's seat. This was going to end badly. At that point I believed I had probably just killed everybody, but I didn't stop. I didn't even slow down.

I made it to within about five yards of the man getting out of the other car before he turned around. It was Rowley. He was pulling a radio transmitter out of his pocket—or was he putting it away? Everything depended on whether he'd contacted Winter or not.

"Sorry, just stopped for a toilet break," I proffered. It wasn't much, but it was all I had. I kept walking as I talked.

"You seem a whole lot out of breath for someone just taking a leak."

He was right.

Enough talking. While he was taking a split second to decide whether to believe me or not, I pulled out my blood-soaked knife and lunged toward him. Rowley was a lot quicker on his feet than his colleague. He stepped to one side, so I ended up thrusting my knife past his torso finding no target at all. He responded by kicking me in the groin, sending me to the ground.

Everything hinged on Rowley going for his gun rather than the transmitter, which had also fallen to the ground. Rowley went for his gun. In a sea of pain, I found my feet, looked him in the eye and feigned to his right with my blade. He fell for it and moved to his left. This is what I expected a professional to do, so I swung the knife across his body and slashed deep into his chest. He dropped his gun.

Most men would have been down at this point, but not Rowley. He grunted, fell backward against the car, bounced off, and charged at me; unfortunately for me, he had reached into his belt and found a knife of his own. Fortunately for me, the man's strength was running out. His chest was soaking red; he was losing a lot of blood. I managed to kick his knife to one side and plunged mine straight into his throat. Rowley looked at me, his face full of surprise, and then emptiness. He fell to the ground, dead.

I took a minute to catch my breath, listening for any sound that would betray Rowley's communication of the discovery of my car. Hearing only the crashing of distant waves at the cliff bottom, I thought I was in the clear. I cleaned myself off as best I could. I was clearly showing the physical signs of being involved in a fight. I hoped the cover of darkness would let that pass unnoticed.

I climbed into my car, started the engine, turned on the lights, and headed to my appointment with Giles Winter.

As I belted along those last few hundred yards of road along the clifftop, I felt no remorse about what I had just done. I would deal with that later. I did, however, feel good about one thing: the odds had just improved some more. They were now five to one, and I was a very coldly determined and pissed off one.

Then I looked at my watch; the timing was too tight.

I was going to be too late to save Jack Greatrex.

# Chapter 32

The Mini skidded to a halt as I came to the battery entrance. I went to run past Winter's man on the main gate but was stopped by a hand on my chest.

"Arms out, feet spread." He was going to search me.

Luckily, I had thrown my knife out the car window before I rounded the last corner. I had expected to be searched, but I couldn't afford the delay.

"At least let Winter know I'm here," I said, pointing to the transmitter in the guard's other hand.

He ignored me and went on patting me down. I kept listening for the sound of the bullet that would end Greatrex's life.

"Go in," instructed the guard.

I raced through the small tunnel under the embankment and onto the parade ground. In that moment, under the light of a cold, merciless moon, I realized I was too late. Across the parade ground near the first gun placement was Giles Winter, pistol in hand. A prone figure was lying awkwardly at his feet. The figure was motionless. I walked toward them, but I already knew who it was. The body lying unmoving on the ground was my best friend, Jack Greatrex.

I felt waves of despair stirring through my very being, I tried to fight it: Leyla, Amira, and Kaitlin needed me to fight it. They needed a strong, calm man, but I did not feel like that man.

"You bastard," I yelled at Winter, not for the first time tonight.

He looked at me. "You pathetic fool," he said. His tone was patronizing. "I haven't even shot him yet. He's still out cold from being knocked on the head by Rowley." Winter seemed mildly amused by the situation. "Your friend must have a very thin skull. He didn't even regain consciousness when we dragged him over here from the car."

Relief enveloped me as I pulled myself together. I would have smiled but I didn't. I would have smiled because at that point I knew exactly what was going on. Greatrex and I had often discussed the strategies we'd use if we were captured while on a mission. He was a strong exponent of the "play dead" school. "If you're knocked down, stay down. People will say more if they think you can't hear." Jack Greatrex was no more unconscious than I was.

I looked down at the stillness of his body. His hands were bound behind his back. Winter's men hadn't thought it was necessary to bind his feet. It was necessary, and I hoped they'd soon learn why.

"Can I check on him?" I asked Winter. Nicholas Sharp, concerned friend.

"Be my guest. Not much point though; you'll both be dead shortly."

Such graciousness.

I got down on my knees, making sure I had my back to Winter. I could hear Greatrex's steady breathing. Pretending I was checking his eyes, I leaned down close to my friend's ear and whispered, "What you'll need is under the gun on the right," referring to one of the packages I had left in my earlier reconnaissance. Jack would know what I meant.

I got up to my feet and turned to face Winter. The guard from the gate had come over to see what was going on. What I needed to do now was get Winter and his man as far away from Greatrex as quickly as I could.

"He'll be out for a while," I said.

"Good for him," said Winter, "although it's a shame he won't feel the bullet when it comes."

What a guy.

Winter then brushed the dark hair from his face and looked me straight in the eye.

"The samples—I presume you have them?"

"I have them," I replied.

"Where? I don't see the package."

"I want to see the girls," I demanded.

Winter then hit me hard across the face.

"You don't make the rules here, Sharp. I thought we'd established that."

"No girls, no samples," I reiterated, waiting for more pain. It came, back of my head, courtesy of Winter's enforcer.

"We've no time for this," said Winter. "I'll take you to them when you tell me where the samples are; if you don't, I'll deal with Jack Greatrex now." He began to raise his gun.

"In my car, under the passenger seat," I responded. I hated bullies, but I hated losing friends more.

I started to walk toward the car, but Winter stopped me with a hand.

"Preston, take care of it," he said to the gate guard.

"Preston" walked off toward the entrance leading to my car.

Winter didn't move. I needed him to move.

"The girls," I said.

Possibly for the first time in his life, Giles Winter kept his word. We started walking toward the tunnel entrance.

It was all I could do not to take a sideways glance at Greatrex, but I looked straight ahead, wanting to keep Winter's mind focused elsewhere.

"So, what will you do with the samples?" I asked.

Winter liked to talk about his work.

"We will reverse engineer them here in England. I have a small group of scientifically skilled British friends. We will then confirm their effectiveness with some small demonstrative attacks."

I felt sick.

"After that, we will move them on to our buyer, or should I say buyers. We have one in Russia and one in the Middle East. This is why we needed you to get them back to England, under military guard of course." He seemed very satisfied with himself. I hated that.

We had reached the tunnel entrance and Winter hadn't looked back. Then he began to turn around.

I pretended to trip and fell against him. He didn't buy it for a second, turning back and lashing my face with the butt of his gun. It hurt like hell, but by then we were on the stairs leading down to the tunnel. Greatrex was out of view.

Winter continued, "You fool, Sharp. You have no choices here. I'm still considering whether your girls live or die; one more pointless move like that will decide it for me."

I knew Winter wasn't deciding anything. He planned to murder us all, here, tonight. The fact he just gave me all that information had confirmed it.

We climbed down the circular stairs to the tunnel floor. Winter made sure I led the way. He then produced a torch and shone its light down a very long brick-lined tunnel. It was more like a corridor. There was comfortable standing room, but only just enough width for two people to pass each other.

"Wait," he said. "We go nowhere until Preston returns with the samples."

Two minutes later, the clamor of feet on the metal stairs above us told us Winter's man had arrived. As he joined us, he held out the package containing the samples.

"They were where he said," Preston nodded in my direction as he spoke.

"Very well," said Winter. "For once you have done something sensible, Sharp. Now you can join your friends." He managed to make even that simple sentence sound sinister.

He shone the light back down the tunnel and pushed me ahead of him.

"Preston, stay here," Winter commanded. "Make sure we are not disturbed."

As we walked along the tunnel, it seemed like we were gradually going downhill. I couldn't help but feel that if Winter had his way, neither I, nor Kaitlin, Amira, or Leyla would be making the return uphill journey. There was a certain irony in the fact that during the day the path we walked was traveled by hordes of tourists, yet here, tonight, it seemed like the most remote and frightening location on earth.

Seconds ticked away. I was aware that by giving the samples over to Winter, I had taken an enormous risk. Any possible control I had over the timing of events was gone. Alternatively, if I hadn't given him the package, I wouldn't have been able to gain access to the girls, not to mention the fact that Winter was itching to start shooting people.

We walked in silence for about 200 feet before I felt a fresh breeze on my face; it seemed to come from the far end of the tunnel. We had rounded several bends so far, but as we rounded the last one, I saw a dim light. We then started going up instead of down.

Two minutes later we walked into a small concrete-lined room. Moonlight shone through iron grates covering an opening in the wall that looked out over the sea. The breeze was stronger now. In the center of the room was a large, aging searchlight, obviously at one time an essential part of the old battery's defense system. My eyes, however, were glued to the sight of the two women and little girl who were sitting on the floor, leaning against the half-wall below the opening. Leyla, Kaitlin, and Amira looked dreadful.

Leyla looked totally worn out. She had bruises on her face and her clothes were torn. Amira sat whimpering next to her mother. Kaitlin had fared no better. She had been a captive of Winter for less time than the others, but from the look of her she had been brutalized, probably while being questioned about my activities. Bruises covered her face, and she had some cuts and burns on her arms.

I felt my temper rise, but I swiftly quelled it as a luxury I could not afford. It was then that I noticed the other two figures in the room: Santori in a shadow to the right, and an unknown enforcer to the left. They both had automatic machine guns trained on the girls. It took me several seconds to speak.

"Leyla, Kaitlin, my little Amira, are you all right?" My voice sounded strained, even to me.

A light flickered in Leyla's eyes when she looked up and saw me. Then, as she looked around the room, it disappeared.

"We are surviving, Nicholas," she answered.

"Will we be okay now?" asked Amira, her voice fragile and weak.

"Of course you will," I said.

I moved forward to hug her, but Santori's fist came out of the shadow and sent me lurching back across the small room.

Amira screamed.

"Weren't you taught not to lie to children, Sharp?" Winter sneered.

Even in this situation he could not allow a little girl a moment of false comfort. At that second, I was certain that if the opportunity arose, I would end Giles Winter's life tonight.

Winter continued, "It is time for me to wish you my condolences and leave." He nodded at Santori and his offsider.

"Wait five minutes, then you know what to do, Santori."

Santori nodded. I didn't like the look on his face.

With that, Winter turned and fled up the tunnel, clutching his precious and deadly package.

The situation appeared hopeless. Winter's two men, each with a rapid-fire weapon, the three girls, worn out, tired beyond caring, and me. I was tired, I was sore, and I had no weapon, but I also had no intention of letting it all end here.

We waited the full five minutes. I counted it out.

Santori waited because he was instructed to. I waited because I wanted to give Greatrex a chance to improve the odds upstairs. I also didn't know quite what I could do down here without endangering the girls any further.

Then, "Do it, Nicholas." Kaitlin spoke for the first time. "There's a chance you may be able to save Amira."

Brave woman. I liked her a lot.

"Shut up," said Santori. He began to raise his weapon.

"I don't need to do anything," I said.

Kaitlin looked confused. So did Leyla. For a fraction of a second Santori looked confused too. That's all it took.

The sound of a gun firing startled everyone, none more so than Santori's offsider, who saw a red patch appear on his arm. In the same second I catapulted myself across the room, grabbing Santori's gun with both hands and sending him to the ground. Out of the corner of my eye, I saw Greatrex barreling around the final tunnel corner and into the room. The gun he had just fired was still in his hand. Greatrex's victim saw him too. Even in his injured state, Winter's man managed to sidestep the big fella's charge and floor Greatrex with a powerful right jab.

I was caught unprepared as I felt Santori's fist smash into the side of my head. I went back against the wall, hitting my head on the concrete. He made a bid for his gun; it was still in my hands, but my grip was weak. As Santori snatched the weapon and raised it to fire, I could see through blurred vision that he wasn't aiming at me. He was aiming at Greatrex, who now seemed to be getting the better of his injured opponent. As I leaped at him for a second time, Santori turned to me and fired, but his shot went wide.

"Get out now," I screamed at the girls. There were too many bullets in an enclosed space for anyone to be safe. "Go now," I repeated.

Leyla and Kaitlin ran up the corridor with Amira between them. I didn't know what was waiting for them at the end of the tunnel, but it would have to be better than this.

It had been a mistake to take my eyes off Santori; he had

regrouped and came at me with a sharp kick to my right knee. It brought me down—the pain was overpowering.

Greatrex must have seen me fall. He had finished off his opponent with a final punch and then dived across the room toward Santori, but the space was too wide for him to cross it in time. Again, Santori lifted his weapon and pointed it at my friend. Greatrex grabbed at the spotlight to his left for cover, but it wasn't going to be enough.

As Santori fired I flicked my good leg out and tripped him. The shot went wide but still collected Greatrex in the shoulder. Jack grunted in pain as he went down. I had one last chance and took it. I sprung up on my single available leg and threw all my weight on Santori. He was looking at Greatrex, so he didn't see me until it was too late. I took him down hard, punching him with as much strength as I could muster as he fell. He dropped the gun. It was out of his reach but just within mine. As I reached for it, Santori clambered to his feet and came at me with a knife that he seemed to produce from out of nowhere. I threw myself out of his way, slamming into the wall again. As Santori turned for another run at me I grabbed the gun, raised it, and fired. My opponent was dead before he hit the ground.

I looked over to Greatrex.

"The girls," I yelled.

Clutching his shoulder, Jack was two steps ahead of me as I limped my way up the tunnel. My knee was causing me grief, but I kept moving. We were each now carrying an AK-47. I was pleased we were properly armed, especially considering the physical state we were both in. We passed the limp body of Winter's man Preston. Greatrex's previous handiwork, I presumed. We ascended the spiral stairs and ran as best we could out onto the parade ground.

I had got three paces into the open when I sensed the gunshot, as much as heard it, as a bullet went whistling over my head.

"Don't even think about moving."

Silhouetted in the moonlight was Elliot Brooks, holding a pistol. If it had been pointing at me, I would have taken my chances and just let loose with my machine gun. But the gun wasn't pointing at me, it was pointing at Amira. Brooks held the little girl around the neck, his gun an inch from the side of her head.

"Drop your weapons, both of you, now," he commanded.

We dropped our guns. The next sound we heard was tires screeching on the road at the other side of the battery entrance. I put two and two together.

"Your faithful pal, Giles Winter, has abandoned you, Brooks. How does it feel?" I shouted across the parade ground.

It was only then I noticed Kaitlin and Leyla in shadow on the ground about ten feet from Brooks and about twenty feet from me. They were alive, but they didn't look good.

"We tried to stop them," said Kaitlin.

Looking at a wound that was bleeding from her thigh I thought she had given it a good go.

"Nick … Amira." Leyla sounded desperate.

My first goal was to get between Brooks and the women.

"Don't be a fool, Brooks. Let her go and you can walk out of here."

"Not a chance, Sharp. If it ends here for me, it ends here for us all."

"I don't think that's how Winter looks at it," I responded as I glanced toward the entrance. As I talked, I walked toward him.

A quick look of frustration crossed his face. It was visible even in the moonlight.

"Not another step, Sharp."

As he spoke, Brooks backed up toward the gun placements, dragging Amira with him.

I stopped. Brooks appeared to have all the cards, because he had that sweet little girl.

I could feel Greatrex behind me, agitating, waiting to push forward.

When in doubt, cause confusion, create misdirection. I learned that at training.

I jumped backward into the shadows near the tunnel entrance.

Brooks was momentarily perplexed.

"That's it—run, hide, you coward. I knew there was nothing to you."

As I hit the shadows, I reached around for one of the packages I'd dropped off earlier. My hands found the cloth, removed it, and grabbed at the revolver. I turned and aimed it in Brooks' direction. I was still out of his sight.

It was a risky shot with only a handgun, but I took it. The sharp sound of the firing gun echoed around the walls of the battery. The bullet found Brooks' right arm. I had needed to aim as far away from Amira as possible. In the time it took Brooks to realize he'd been hit, Greatrex charged across the parade ground like a madman, first putting himself between Brooks and the women and then continuing his assault. Unfortunately, Brooks had not dropped his gun, even after being shot. He passed it to his other hand, held it up, and pointed it at Greatrex. The big fella stopped dead in his tracks;

he had no choice.

"Looks like we've both been abandoned," Greatrex shouted, looking directly at Brooks. "Let's talk this through." Jack was buying time.

Although Brooks had the gun in his left hand, his arm was still around Amira's neck.

"That may well be, but I'm leaving here with this child. What you do now will decide whether she lives or dies."

Then Brooks broke out his despicably condescending smile. He shouldn't have done that.

I had managed to stay in the shadows and work my way around to the furthest gun placement. There were half-walls between each of them. I could easily conceal myself as I moved closer.

Greatrex kept Brooks focused ahead of him as I came around the last wall behind him. I lunged forward and knocked Brooks to the ground. He released his hold on Amira to break his own fall. The stubborn bastard still hadn't dropped his gun. We had both hit the ground, but he got up more quickly than me. He aimed the gun at me and started to squeeze the trigger.

He didn't finish. Greatrex had closed the remaining distance in an instant. He grabbed Brooks around the neck. I grabbed Amira and threw her into her mother's arms. For a minute Greatrex and Brooks struggled. I couldn't see a way to get in and help. Next thing, Greatrex lifted Elliot Brooks above his head and threw him over the wall of the gun placement and over the cliff edge, not a bad feat for a man with a bullet in his shoulder. Brooks' tortured scream was the last sound we heard as he fell hundreds of feet to the rocks below.

Then Jack Greatrex collapsed.

"See to him. Don't let him bleed out," I shouted to the girls. Amira was sobbing in her mother's arms. Kaitlin ran toward Greatrex, ripping her shirt off as she ran. Any bandage would do.

I had no choice in what I had to do next. A very bad man was getting away with a weapon that could hurt, maim, or kill thousands of people, and I had given it to him.

I planned to get it back.

Dragging my injured leg behind me, I hobbled as fast as I could through the battery entrance and into the car park. The black Mini was where I had left it; I climbed in and pressed the starter. Nothing. Winter's man had taken the key. Damn!

I looked around. Across the car park was the Ford we had pursued across the island, Brooks' car. I made my way over to it. I was getting desperate; every second was vital if I was to catch up with Winter. The altercation with Brooks had cost precious minutes. I climbed in—the key was there. I started the engine and floored the accelerator as I sped down the track toward the road.

A few seconds later I hit the asphalt road that ran across the top of the cliffs and turned onto it. I paused for a second to see if I could locate Winter's car, or at least his lights along the dark winding road. In that moment, when I saw the car lights, my heart sank. There was only one car on the road; it had to be Winter, but he was way too far along. I would never catch him, not a chance. I had failed. Giles Winter was going to get away. He was going to be able to spread more fear and death, and it was going to be my fault.

I was attempting to hold back tears of frustration and anger as I surveyed the scene in front of me. In the bright moonlight I could see it all so clearly. Winter had been clever. Winter was always clever. The man had his escape route planned out well in advance. As his car wound down the distant cliff road, I could see he was almost at sea level. At the end of the road Winter sped along was a jetty protruding into the bay. At the end of the jetty was a boat, a fast-looking half-cabin with two large outboard engines on its stern. I then looked across the bay and saw the bigger picture. The dark silhouette of a large motor yacht with all its running lights turned off appeared stationary just off the headland. It didn't take much to figure out Winter's strategy. He was going use the boat at the jetty to get to the yacht and then disappear.

It seemed like a slow-motion dream as I watched Winter climb out of his car and run along the jetty. The light from the almost full moon was so bright I could even make out what I assumed to be the package of chemical weapon samples clutched under his arm. Where were they going to end up? "Demonstrative attacks," he had said. Who was going to die? … Who was going to die … because of me?

I just sat there in the driver's seat of Brooks' car, helpless, defeated, and beyond frustrated. I looked around me, as if someone, something, anything could help. There was nothing. It seemed like forever, but it was probably not more than a minute that I sat there and watched Winter climb onto the boat from the jetty. I pounded the steering wheel in anger.

I looked behind me, as if waiting for the cavalry to come over the hill. And there it was—not the cavalry, but a glimmer of hope. I should have noticed it earlier. Lying on the back seat was a soft case. In it would be the rifle that Elliot Brooks used at the festival. Perhaps there was a chance.

I wasted no time. I jumped out of the car, opened the rear door, and pulled Brooks' case out. I could feel the sweat pouring down my forehead as I ripped it open. Then, there it was, the familiar shape of an M40A5 bolt-action sniper rifle. I frantically pulled it out.

The urgency was overwhelming. The big question now was ammunition. Did the rifle have any? Surely, Brooks would not be so egotistical to think he would only need one bullet when he attempted to take Robbie West's life. I pulled out the detachable box magazine. Brooks had been egotistical; he had thought he would only need two bullets at most. There was one round left.

I reloaded the magazine and ran around the front of the car to the cliff edge. There was no bipod to steady the rifle, so I grabbed a decent-sized rock and lay down on the ground. Resting the long barrel of the M40 on the rock, I looked through the familiar AN/PVS universal night sight, which allowed me to focus far ahead across the waves to Winter's boat. He had left the jetty and was heading toward the dark outline of the yacht. I wouldn't have long to make this work, if I could make it work. Winter was heading north, away from me. Every second counted. The boat looked to be around one thousand yards away. The accurate range of the rifle was around eleven hundred yards. I would have about twenty seconds to take the shot, twenty-five at most. I felt my heart pounding like a hammer in my chest.

The wind had picked up to around fifteen knots. I would have to take that into account. It didn't help my chances any. Winter's boat was going into the chop of the waves, white-capped crests of water surrounding it. I would have to time the shot and my breathing with the movement of the waves. I rated my chances of success at around two percent, but two percent was better than none.

I slowed down my breathing and began to feel the rhythm of the waves as the boat moved through them. I needed to make the shot in the space between exhaling and inhaling to keep the rifle barrel steady. I was soaked in sweat, and my nerves felt as though they were ready to explode.

Then he was there. I had Winter in my sights, my hands were rock steady—no nerves this time, not like a few days before in Iraq. That surprised me.

Breathe slowly, easily. The boat rises, the boat falls, wave by wave. Breathe out steadily. I thought briefly of Akram Salib. I thought of the terror on Amira's face when Winter held a gun to her head. I thought also of the people who would die if Giles Winter lived. I slowly finished exhaling, my sights were on the back of Winter's head. I counted one, two ... and squeezed the trigger.

The sound of the shot echoed through the night, but I kept looking through the sight. I saw Giles Winter fall sideways and slump against the controls of his boat. I had him. As relief poured through me, I started shaking. It was difficult to keep my sights on the boat, but I tracked its path.

The bow seemed to rise and increase in speed as Winter fell. It was hurtling over the waves now, being thrown in the air and landing precariously again and again. It was clear that Winter was either dead or totally incapacitated. No one was controlling that boat now. Then, to my surprise, it began to veer left, tracing a large arc and heading toward the rocks at the bottom of the chalk cliff face below me and to my left.

The boat was traveling faster and faster; it seemed to be spending as much time in the air as in the water. I could hear the twin engines over-revving; emitting a piercing metallic screech.

One hundred feet, fifty feet, twenty-five, and then … the explosion was monstrous. Flames leaped forty feet in the air. The fuel tanks had ignited on impact as Giles Winter and his boat simply ceased to exist. Then it hit me—that meant the chemical weapon and nerve agent samples would have been incinerated.

I stared at where the boat used to be for what seemed like an eternity. One shot, one moment, one bullet. It was over.

I started to laugh. It seemed like forever since I had laughed. Was I losing it? Probably, but I didn't care. Was I relieved? Yes, big-time. I rolled over and lay on my back, still laughing, maybe crying too. The tears of a madman. After a few minutes I began to calm down and my breathing slowed. As I lay there on the clifftop, staring up at the night sky, the wind and the waves became a soundtrack to some sort of distorted, introspective film playing over and over in my head. The trouble was, I couldn't seem to follow the narrative.

I could have sworn the stars in the dark sky above were laughing at me.

# Epilogue

The elaborate black wrought-iron gates stood in front of us, supported either side by stone pillars the size of monuments. Behind the gates was a long, winding, tree-lined drive. Lush green fields divided by gleaming white post-and-rail fences completed the fairy-tale picture.

From the gate, you couldn't see the house.

I glanced over at Jack Greatrex. He was sitting next to me, sharing the rear seat of the limousine. Jack was looking well now; his shoulder had healed. He was a little stiff, but was doing okay. It was six weeks since the death of Giles Winter at the foot of those chalk cliffs on the Isle of Wight.

A few days earlier we had been sitting at Medina's Bar having a quiet drink, reflecting on the events of the previous weeks, when both our phones had buzzed simultaneously. I had looked down at mine; there was a message that read, "See you next Monday, 2 p.m., my place, a car will pick you up at the airport." It was signed Colin Devlin-Waters. The general. There was an attachment; it was an air ticket to Washington. Greatrex had received the same message.

A few days previously I had taken Leyla and Amira back to Portland and made sure they were safe and secure. I had tried to persuade Leyla to move them to LA to be closer to Greatrex and I, but she had insisted that she and Amira had built their new life in Portland; it was their home now.

After installing state-of-the-art surveillance cameras outside their home and employing a security firm to check on them regularly, I headed back to the City of Angels. Amira's resilience was amazing. She was an impressive little girl, but it would still take the two of them a long time to get over their ordeal.

Greatrex and I had nothing booked for the following week, so we took the general up on his invitation—or was it a summons? Either way, here we were, in rural Maryland, waiting at these grand entrance gates. The driver spoke into an intercom, and the gates opened.

"I was thinking of an apartment in a good area of Washington," said Greatrex, "not something like this."

As he spoke, we rounded the last bend in the drive, revealing a magnificent two-story brick and wood residence, abundant with porches and painted in light gray.

"Wow," I said. Nicholas Sharp, master of eloquent understatement.

The car stopped, we climbed out, and walked up onto the landing that surrounded the oversized wooden front doors. Before we could knock, the doors opened, and there she stood, Kaitlin, her blonde hair tumbling around her shoulders and her face glowing. She looked very different to that final night in England.

"My stepfather is expecting you," she said as she gave me a lingering kiss on the lips. We had seen each other several times over the last few weeks and had grown closer. I was enjoying that.

Kaitlin must have noticed or even expected our wide-eyed

glances around the huge entrance hall as we walked through the doorway.

"Impressive isn't it," she said, as if answering the question we hadn't dared ask out loud. "It's the 'Devlin' part of 'Devlin-Waters,'" she said. "Old money, and a lot of it. My stepfather refused to just sit back and take something for nothing; that's why he joined the Marines, to prove he was his own man."

Kaitlin paused thoughtfully for a moment. "I think that's what attracted my mother to him, that stubborn independence, the need to do things his own way."

Both Greatrex and I nodded; that certainly summed up the general.

Kaitlin led us down a long, wide corridor and indicated a door to the right.

"Go on in." She gave us a knowing grin as she opened the door. "I'll join you later."

The room we entered was a large traditional study. Chesterfield-style sofas, an enormous classic wooden desk, and bookshelves everywhere. It was dimly lit by expensive-looking lamps scattered around the space. Behind the desk was the familiar figure of the general. It was the first time we had seen him in person since our return.

He got up, stepped around the desk, and came forward to greet us.

"Nicholas, Jack, wonderful to see you," he said as he shook our hands. H sounded like he meant it. "No loud sandstorms to have to yell over here," he said, referring to our last meeting at the Al Taji Base. "Now, before we talk, I'd like to introduce you to a couple of old friends."

I hadn't noticed the two figures sitting in comfortable lounge chairs in one corner of the room. They got up and turned to face us.

"Speechless" is an overused word, but in this case both Jack Greatrex and I had nothing, no words at all. Before us we saw two very familiar faces, although they belonged to two men we had never met. I'd seen them on television, read about them, and heard them interviewed.

"I don't believe you gentlemen have met," said the general.

He introduced us. We all shook hands.

I looked over at Greatrex; if he was in shock, he was taking it in his stride.

"Please, everyone, have a seat," offered the general.

We all sat on the two large sofas, with the general sitting to one side on a very comfortable-looking winged armchair.

"Well," began the familiar Texan drawl of the man sitting opposite me. "We asked Colin to arrange an opportunity to speak to you two gentlemen in person, but privately. I hope that's okay with you?"

"We would like to thank you, thank you for everything you have done," interrupted his colleague. I always appreciated the inflections of a classic British accent.

Before either Greatrex or I could get a word out, the American continued. "We know that you have risked your own lives to save not only those of your friends, but of countless others. While there can be no official recognition, we wanted you to know how much your efforts have been appreciated."

"Several years ago, in our previous roles, we were both involved in making some decisions that affected a lot of people," said the Brit, nodding at his US counterpart. "They were decisions that have since been challenged and derided in the media and around the world, although given the information available to the public at the time, we both find that understandable."

"The thing is," the American took over, "our people on the ground always thought we were right. We knew that Saddam had those chemical weapons, but we just couldn't prove it. Our teams searched thoroughly but found nothing. Of course, we had no concept of what Giles Winter and his organization had put in play. They had made sure our search would be fruitless. The result was our respective countries ended up looking like we had provoked a needless war."

I looked over at the general. He said nothing but sat back with a small grin on his face, enjoying the show.

"We know this can never be made public knowledge," continued the Brit, "but because of what you found and destroyed—those samples and formulas—we, and the people we worked with, can rest a little easier about the decisions that were made back then."

"Quite simply, Mr. Sharp and Mr. Greatrex, we thank you," said the American.

With that they both got up, shook our hands, and walked out of the room.

The general was still grinning.

An hour and a half later we had finished sharing an expansive lunch and a full debrief with the general and his stepdaughter. There were still some unanswered questions, including the strength and depth of Giles Winter's links to the British. "We may never know," had been the general's perspective.

As we strolled around the estate's manicured gardens, the general touched me on the arm. I stopped and turned to look at him. Greatrex and Kaitlin, a little ahead of us, stopped as well.

"I want to ask you something, Nicholas," began the general.

"I would like to know if something comes up again, a situation in which your skills could be helpful, can I call on you?"

If ever there was such a thing as a fully loaded question, this was it.

I looked out over the rolling green fields of rural Maryland; it was so peaceful. My thoughts went to the people who had recently met their deaths at my hands. They were clearly bad men, but Greatrex and I were still the ones who had been called on to end their lives. That was a heavy weight. I thought of Giles Winter and the evil he was going to unleash on so many innocent people. We had protected those people.

There were unanswered questions and unresolved issues that I had been persistently pushing away. It gradually dawned on me that I could hide no more. I still had one more battle to fight, but this skirmish was to be fought deep within my soul.

When this all began, I was sure I was reluctant to be drawn back into the dusky world of death and violence I had once abandoned. I had believed I had no choice but to walk this road one last time. Now I was not so sure; in fact, I was deeply unsure. In the end, I had separated my actions from my emotions all too easily. I had killed too easily.

I remembered laying on that clifftop staring at the stars, searching for clarity.

I wondered, was it too convenient to blame everything that had come to pass solely on Giles Winter? For certain, Winter was the most evil being I had ever encountered, and stopping him was the right thing to do, but perhaps there was more to this. What emotional layer had been lying deep within me? Was it badness, restlessness, goodness, recklessness? I didn't really know, but it had been dormant, and now it wasn't. Was there some small amount of evil in me that needed to be there, so I could effectively help and protect? Did I want to do this? Did I need to do this?

I turned toward the general. He was looking me straight in the eye, as if trying to read my thoughts. I looked over his shoulder; Kaitlin was doing the same thing.

I returned my gaze to the safety of the hills. I thought of my relatively new life as a creative. That was my world now. Again, my mind went back to that clifftop on the Isle of Wight—the manic laughter, the inexplicable tears, the conflict I'd felt. There had been no resolution. I had not yet found the clarity I sought.

Lastly, I looked at Jack Greatrex, my friend, the man who had always had my back. He looked at me and shrugged, no damn help at all.

"Well?" the general deserved an answer.

"I don't know," I said. "I simply do not know."

# Afterword

**Get your FREE electronic copy of the NICHOLAS SHARP origins Novella PLAY OUT, the latest news about new releases and some other exciting freebies along the way by joining my mailing list at my website: https://markmannock.com**

Although you can begin reading the NICHOLAS SHARP THRILLER series at any point here is my suggested order of reading:

1. **KILLSONG** (NS thriller No. 1-*available on Amazon*)
2. **BLOOD NOTE** (A NS short story-*available exclusively to my mailing list members. I'll send you the link 7 days after sign-up*)
3. **LETHAL SCORE** (NS thriller No. 2-*available on Amazon*)
4. **HELL'S CHOIR** (NS thriller No. 3-*available on Amazon September 2020*)

**PLAY OUT**-an origins novella (*available exclusively to my mailing list members on sign-up*) can be read at any point. The story takes you back to when Nicholas Sharp left the U.S. Marines.

**Reviews are life's blood to an author**.  If you've enjoyed **KILLSONG** please consider leaving a review on the book's Amazon page.

## Acknowledgements

My heartfelt thanks and love to Sarah, Anisha and Jack for your love, tolerance and support.  Lachlan, your counsel and wisdom has always been appreciated. Tony Ryan, editor extraordinaire. Thank you so much.

*Cover by Anisha Mannock*

# About the Author

Mark Mannock was born in Melbourne, Australia. He has had an extensive career in the music industry including supporting, recording with or writing for Tina Turner, Joni Mitchell, The Eurythmics, Irene Cara and David Hudson. His recorded work with Lia Scallon has twice been long-listed for Grammy Awards. As a composer/songwriter Mark's music has been used across the world in countless television and theatre contexts, including the 'American Survivor' TV series and 'Sleuth' playwright Anthony Shaffer's later productions.

Mark is presently writing the 'Nicholas Sharp' thriller series about a disillusioned former US sniper whose past plagues him as he makes his way in the contemporary music industry. Sharp is a man whose insatiable curiosity and embedded moral compass lead him to places he ought not go. The series is currently read in over 50 countries.

Mark lives on Victoria's Mornington Peninsula with his family. His travels around the globe act as inspirations for his writing.

Mark enjoys hearing from his readers, so please feel free to contact him.

**You can connect with me on:**

🌐 https://markmannock.com

📘 https://www.facebook.com/markmannockbooks

**Subscribe to my newsletter:**

✉ https://markmannock.com

# Also by Mark Mannock

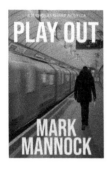

**PLAY OUT**
**A Nicholas Sharp Origin Novella**

***Sign up to my mailing list and receive this book for free!***

Set five years before **KILLSONG**
   **A Terrorist attack on the London Underground. Nicholas Sharp doesn't think so.**

While on leave from Iraq, the U.S. Marine Sniper finds himself intervening when innocent lives are threatened. He walks away, but for Sharp it's never that easy. Something doesn't feel right. Twenty-four hours later everything is wrong.

The brief solace he finds in his beloved piano is shattered when Sharp becomes the attacker's next target. Step up or step away. Nicholas Sharp doesn't like to kill, but he sure as hell knows how to.

**Somewhere between Lee Child's *Jack Reacher* and Robert Crais' *Elvis Cole*, Nicholas Sharp may be a flawed human, but you certainly want him on your side.**

## LETHAL SCORE

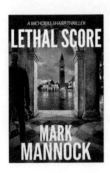

*Nicholas Sharp Thriller Number 2*

**How could he not follow the girl as she broke into the nuclear power station? Is it even possible for Nicholas Sharp to turn his back when lives are in danger?**

Sharp is on a tour through Europe, the concerts are sold out and the former Marine sniper turned musician is living in luxury thanks to promoter Antonio Ascardi.

Suddenly it all goes wrong. People are dying along the way and Sharp is blamed. Now a hunted man, accused of terrorist crimes across the continent, Nicholas Sharp must fight for his life and freedom.

***Available on Amazon***

## HELL'S CHOIR
*Nicholas Sharp Thriller Number 3*

**A goodwill visit to Sudan, what could possibly go wrong?**

Nicholas Sharp is performing as part of a political and cultural group representing the U.S.. Suddenly caught up in the middle of a political coup, the leader of the American contingent, who also happens to be Vice President of the United States, goes missing and his security staff murdered.

Communication with the outside world is cut off. It falls to Sharp and Greatrex to track their missing leader down.

But then things get really complicated…

*Available on Amazon September- 2020*

**BLOOD NOTE**

**A Short Story Prequel to the Thriller KILLSONG** *(should be read after KILLSONG-available FREE to mailing list subscribers 7 days after sign-up)*

**Just turn around and walk away. That was all Nicholas Sharp had to do when the mysterious and intoxicating Elena approached him for help.**

She knew far too much about him. The warning signs were all there.

Sharp didn't listen to them.

What followed for the former Marine Sniper turned musician, was a harrowing night of violence, deceit and intrigue.

When the sunrise ushered in a new day, Sharp thought it was all over…but it was really just beginning.

Lightning Source UK Ltd.
Milton Keynes UK
UKHW010714070421
381574UK00003B/1013